CW00496446

The Switch

The Switch

marvin thomas

Copyright © 2010 Marvin Thomas

The moral right of the author has been asserted.

Apart from any fair dealing for the purposes of research or private study,
or criticism or review, as permitted under the Copyright, Designs and Patents
Act 1988, this publication may only be reproduced, stored or transmitted, in
any form or by any means, with the prior permission in writing of the
publishers, or in the case of reprographic reproduction in accordance with
the terms of licences issued by the Copyright Licensing Agency. Enquiries
concerning reproduction outside those terms should be sent to the publishers.

Matador
5 Weir Road
Kibworth Beauchamp
Leicester LE8 0LQ, UK
Tel: (+44) 116 279 2299
Fax: (+44) 116 279 2277
Email: books@troubador.co.uk
Web: www.troubador.co.uk/matador

ISBN 978 1848762 374

British Library Cataloguing in Publication Data.
A catalogue record for this book is available from the British Library.

Typeset in 11pt Palatino by Troubador Publishing Ltd, Leicester, UK

Matador is an imprint of Troubador Publishing Ltd

Natasha
Tashana
Tashina
My Life…

I

Hi, my name is Sonny. I own a bar in Manner's Street, Wellington, New Zealand but I'm originally from Havana in Cuba. I've travelled a lot and you'll probably wonder how an illegal immigrant could make it from Cuba to New Zealand and actually make something of himself. Well, it wasn't easy. I spent a little time labouring and a little time in hotels trying to make an honest living. However, after getting caught up with the wrong side of what we have subconsciously called 'the law' I spent most of my time dodging what most people would call 'the unlikely law'; you know, the type of guys who've got badges and guns but would rather be baddies than the law-abiding men of society, which is how we've been taught to acknowledge them. Not to mention PIGS and other derogatory slang. Anyway, on my travels I met a guy named Ian and let me say that in all my days I have never met someone so intriguing, a heart so pure, someone so at one with nature. He is truly a remarkable being. He has power, good and not so good, and he's a force that cannot conflate nor conform. He went through a lot in his time, you could tell. Not just from his story, but from his deep convoluted eyes, which are just unexplainable. I guess it's the old question, bad turning good and people wondering why.

I'm going to tell the man's story as I heard it, felt it and believed it. I think I'll call it *The Switch* as you know the guy's name was Ian. When Ian was about six months old his dad took him away from his mum and brought him to live with *his* mum, Ian's grandma, for her to raise him. However, after a couple of days his dad disappeared. Ian's dad was a small time crook so he always lived underground and his disappearances weren't unusual.

Ian was now being cared for by his grandma and granddad although his granddad was blind and his grandma was very ill. Nevertheless, they took care of him and tried their best to raise him properly, teaching him what they knew about right and wrong. They were very poor and didn't have many possessions; indeed, many a night went by when they would go to bed without food because they simply didn't have any. At that time, Ian was too young to understand. He knew only that sometimes he was hungry and other times he was thirsty. He just accepted what he was given. But when Ian was about three years old, he realised that if he was hungry and there was no food at home he could walk next door and they would give him a snack or a drink. When they didn't do so he would take it or

2

whatever was available; his survival instincts were being fine tuned everyday, he had learnt to do what he had to do to survive.

When Ian was about six his granddad died leaving just him and his grandma. This was a momentous time for Ian and probably one of the greatest feelings he had ever experienced, for it was the first time in his life he was able to wear shoes. He felt great, different, he felt like somebody. The next door neighbour brought them over. They were her son's. She also brought Ian some clothes, those that couldn't fit her boys anymore. He wished the day would never end, it was something to remember.

But despite all the gifts and special treatment, Ian was sad about the death of his granddad. He was blind, but his love for Ian could have seen through a vault door. Ian had loved him also. He did anything his granddad asked of him, even if it meant ridicule from the other children in his class. For example, he would go to school in ragged clothes and sore bare feet, always giving the kids a reason to laugh at him. What could he do? But his grandparents always tried their best for him.

Ian never saw his dad and his dad never sent any money for his grandparents. In fact, no one knew if his dad was dead or alive. He didn't grow up with his mum, so he never knew or saw her and when he was about eight years old his grandmother died. If Ian didn't know how hard life was before then he certainly did now. It was just him, living alone in a small, one-roomed house. He would do different things for a little cash; his neighbours would give him bits and pieces to do for a little pocket money but it was tough for a little kid to be living on his own. There were days when he would have loved to have eaten chicken but he never had any money. He started to collect bottles and things that could be recycled, from his neighbours, knowing he could get a few dollars from doing so. He would go to parties and dances just to get some food to eat. He had to do what he had to do in order to survive. Then life became really tough; he had to stop going to school and find work. He had to do this and that, anything to make some money. In his heart, Ian didn't know who he really was. He didn't have anybody to depend on and no one to tell him where he was from. He didn't know where his mum and dad were and neither had ever tried to contact him, but he knew he couldn't give up. He started a life of crime, he decided to steal and sell.

When Ian was around 12 he met an old lady who said she had a friend who needed someone to take care of her house, so he went and saw them. They were American and had recently moved from Lake Hamilton in Arkansas. Their parents were originally from Jamaica, and since they were now nearing retirement age they thought they would go back to their roots. They had family in the area but their immediate family, children and siblings remained in Arkansas and they made frequent trips back there every year. The house they had bought was a castle compared to Ian's one-roomed house; it had seven bedrooms and three floors, the top floor being more of a sun roof but it also had a living space and a bathroom. The house was rendered to perfection, which was rare in those days. You could tell that a lot of time and money had gone into building the house. The floors were not imported marble, they were tiled with gracious designs and every part of the décor, furniture and fabrics converged. Cyril and Beverley were kind-hearted people who believed that everyone should be given a chance and they decided Ian was no exception. They gave him a place to stay, somewhere to call home. Because it was just the three of them, most of the time Ian felt as though he had the house to himself. He started to look upon Cyril as a father figure. They sent him back to school although he still couldn't read and the kids at school made it hard for him, teasing him and excluding him from games. Indeed, Ian would get into a lot of fights. At home he took care of the house and made sure everything was well looked after. He would do anything he was asked to do and would keep on doing it. But deep down inside crime was calling him. He started to wonder what he would do when he grew up. When the 'Americans', as Ian called them, were away from home, he would remain in the house and keep things perfect. He stayed on his own and cooked his own dinner. Cooking made him feel good; he felt free from his everyday thoughts, worries and lows. There was just him and the food, no rights, no wrongs. No one knew Ian could cook like that; he only entered the kitchen to clean up when the Americans were around. He kept it to himself, it was his secret.

It was by the will of God that Ian was invited to do some building work with the Americans' neighbour, Frank. Frank was of medium height, had sunset-coloured long straight hair and was as black as a blueberry with grey eyes. He had the strong features of an African. Ian wasn't sure about Frank; he had never seen anybody who looked like that, on the island or on TV. It was as though Frank had fallen apart. His people went to a supermarket, picked up what they liked and, well, just put him back together again with no respect for his culture, heritage or personality. The worst thing about Frank was that he had lived in Jamaica for 30 years, same road, same house and he still spoke with an Irish accent. He could be understood by others but they had to talk slowly so he could understand them. Something just didn't add up. Ian was always cautious around Frank, but he didn't want to disrespect the neighbours of the Americans, they had done a lot for him, more than they could possibly ever know.

Frank bought bits of land all over the island and built houses, schools and shops on them. When he said, "the time is right", this usually meant when the government, investors or local people needed to be seen as doing something worthwhile for the community. Frank would benefit hugely from these situations just by developing his own land. In fact, I never knew what Ian meant when he said, "people live the high life for free" until rethinking it over and over and over. Frank had people come and go, buying, giving, cooking, washing, cleaning, driving and he never gave them a penny. In fact, they refused it. Those who did work for him were paid with the money that the government gave him to develop the land; he obviously kept a huge part for himself. The only thing Frank did was invite everyone up to his house on July 2nd. There they would tell Frank what they had been hoping or praying for, good things, they were peaceful and God loving. Ian didn't know what Frank did to make these things happen, but they did. He kept his distance but showed gratitude for the work Frank offered him. Ian had never done building work before but he was happy to accept the challenge and complete whatever the cost. He would watch guys as they lay one block on top of another and Ian stepped into the job with ease, like a fish to water. It was simple work for Ian. He became a master at it and from there a great builder.

Life was looking good. Ian was about 13 and when he looked at himself he felt positive; he was working, making lots of money, had a stable place to live, and crime was the last thing on his mind. Yes, things were looking up.

A year later life took a turn for him, one that he didn't expect. Clarisa, a 14-year-old girl he was dating, became pregnant. She didn't have any family and slept in the back room of a shop that Frank owned. Clarisa would open and close the shop for Frank and clean it and, in return, he would allow her to stay there. Obviously, she also acted as security for the shop as no one would break in if they knew someone was there. It didn't dawn on Ian straight away that Clarisa's pregnancy was a bad thing. He felt remarkable, for him it was a chance to start life all over again and he seized the opportunity. Cyril and Beverley were a little disappointed, but embraced Ian as always and allowed him and Clarisa to stay in the outhouse in readiness for the arrival of the baby and becoming a family. Ian was ready for his new role in life and regarded it as a blessing. Hope was born at 12 o'clock in the afternoon of July 2nd. She was healthy, strong and beautiful – just like her mother. Ian felt proud of her. He worked like a man, earned a man's wage and now he felt like a man. At that young age it was tough for Ian but he still did what he had to do. He did more than just survive; now, like a dad, he wasn't going to give up. He still thought about things he could do to provide for his family. Ian's new skill enabled him to work day and night and make money. But at that time he didn't know what he wanted to do with his life. He never saw Clarisa or Hope, they were always asleep when he got home or out when he woke. He didn't see what he was working for anymore. He just lived each day as it came and had become a dad at a young age. He still couldn't read and write but was good at what he did. Something just wasn't right. The bad thoughts and crime-filled dreams were returning. He couldn't continue to live like that. What was the point? It just wasn't enough for Ian. Eventually he left Clarisa and Hope and went back to the family house where he'd grown up.

The house was a complete mess, almost derelict, with no roof and no doors. In fact, it looked as though no one had ever lived there. It was just a shell with nothing to remind him of his parents or grandparents. This didn't discourage Ian, however; it was another challenge. That's what made everything worthwhile for him.

It took Ian a solid four weeks to put the house back together again. Everything was new and what wasn't new looked new. There were some things that Ian made from scratch – with his own hands. Some nights he didn't sleep; he would work through the night until it was time to go to work. When the house was finished Ian started to get lots of offers from passers-by and neighbours. Of course, Frank took the credit for the outstanding workmanship but this didn't faze Ian. He just went along with whatever the rumour was. Ian knew in his heart what he'd gone through during those four weeks. When he returned home from work the first day after the house was finished and realised there was nothing left for him to do in the house, he felt warm. He sat in the doorway and reminisced about his grandparents and the first time he wore shoes. Even though he hated it now, he remembered how the smell of cornmeal porridge would make him feel safe and secure, like there was nothing to worry about. Although times were hard he had always felt blessed and cared for.

In his spare time, Ian would fix gadgets and appliances. He was a mechanical whizz-kid who could fix anything from televisions to head gaskets. Ian didn't know this until he moved in with the Americans. He always felt confident enough to do it but had never been given the opportunity. The Americans had only the best, but occasionally something would stop dead or smoke out. Beverley would insist that it was broken and that they needed to get a new one imported. Cyril would agree, of course, but then pass it on to Ian to fix and give him the money.

Nobody taught Ian how to do these things. He was born with it; it was a gift from God. He could drive anything on wheels. He was a master when it came to motorbikes, they were his favourite. At weekends he would race old cars and customise monster trucks. When he was in the driving seat he always felt invincible, he used to think that one day he would become a racing car driver. But that wasn't his real desire. Ever since he was a kid his desire was to become an outlaw or, to be more precise, a hired assassin. Of course, he didn't discuss this with anybody. He was a simple guy who kept himself to himself.

During this time Ian and Clarisa still saw each other. It seemed the only difference was that they lived apart. Clarisa put a lot more effort into their relationship but she was very distant with Ian. As always, this never used to bother Ian but now they lived apart he could see it more. He worked hard, while believing that his relationship with Clarisa was a good one and that he didn't have to show any emotion. Ian further believed that she never wanted the hugs and kisses that most girls wanted at night. He was cool with that but now he assessed her distance as some kind of spell, as though she really wasn't there. It was strange and Ian was really confused by it. As far as he was concerned he had a kid and he looked after the kid. He didn't show any emotions. He didn't know how to show them, he wasn't brought up that way. His grandparents were brilliant but life was tough.

Ian's outlook, therefore, was that love didn't bring money into the house, it didn't pay the bills, it didn't put food on the table and it certainly didn't stop the pain his grandparents felt when they saw their children suffer and disappear from their hearts. In fact, when Ian was with Hope he felt even more lost. He didn't know who he was.

As time passed Ian became comfortable – too comfortable – and the days had become predictable and mundane. He asked himself what he was doing. He got up one day and told the people around him that he was leaving and went to see the Americans to tell them he was blessed to have ever been a part of their lives. Beverley cried as though she was losing a son but Cyril was as cool as ever. He shook Ian's hand and led him to the gate with his other arm around his shoulder. He had loved Ian from the beginning, and was proud of the man that he was becoming. Cyril wasn't always sure of the decisions that Ian was making but he always stood by him regardless. Clarisa and Hope waved Ian off and Clarisa decided the two of them should remain in the outhouse. Beverley insisted on it. She refused to lose Hope as well and looked after the girls as though they were her own. Ian allowed his neighbour's son to stay in the house with his family. He knew they would not neglect their new home and he never saw himself coming back so it would be pointless leaving it empty again.

Ian soon found a little place on the beach on the other side of the island, far from what he knew and where he felt comfortable. To pass the time, Ian started making things – dolls and jewellery. It kept his mind occupied. Ian wasn't a hustler, he didn't beg for custom or attention from the tourists. They approached him and gave him what they felt the souvenir was worth. Some people were very generous and others, well, let's just say it always evened out thanks to the generous ones.

Ian took to diving. He loved it and like just about everything else in his life, he didn't know that he was a terrific swimmer, it was another clash with the elements. Ian felt he could combat anything. Sometimes, when the tourist bus boats came by, he would swim for them and do extravagant dives from ten metres high and sometimes more. He would get a lot of money from this and save his best dives for the yachts, and private catamarans. Ian knew these people only came to see him dive. Building work was short on that side of the island so this was Ian's main income. He wasn't worried, he made enough to send to Clarisa and Hope and still had plenty left over.

Ian was always meeting foreigners on the beach. They amused him. Some of the people he noticed would go and return to the island two, maybe three, times a year. He'd call them 'Mr & Mrs Too Rich'. One lady in particular, an English lady in her forties, was nice. He enjoyed talking to her as she was caring and down to earth. She told him about England, the weather, the education, the Queen, stuff that meant nothing to Ian, but he was still happy to listen. Somehow she calmed his spirit. The world just seemed a better place when she spoke. He hoped that one day he could make the trip to England but that was deep in the back of his mind for the time being. In any case, he only felt like that when Sarah was talking. As far as Ian was concerned he had a daughter and a lot of things to do and achieve in Jamaica, so he decided to take one step at a time. In due course, Ian and Sarah got involved. Sarah hoped Ian would change his mind about going to England but life for him was okay so why rock the boat? He was certain he would stay in Jamaica, he was sure he didn't want to leave. She kept asking him but it soon turned into a game, with smart replies from Ian.

A year had gone by but just as Sarah was resigned to being disappointed, she received a call from Ian. It turned out he was wanted by the law. Hope was walking to the corner shop and was stopped by a man from the neighbourhood who wanted her to follow him home. When she said no, the man tried to force her into the car, touching her up, ripping her school blouse and popping the button off her school skirt. Hope kicked and screamed and drew attention to the situation. The man pushed her and she landed in the bush at the side of the road. Bruised and scared, Hope lay on the bed; she was hurt, not just physically but emotionally too. She didn't move from her bed until Ian arrived. When she saw him she rose up, as though Ian's presence in the room gave her energy. She felt better and when he left she continued as though nothing had ever happened. Ian had taken her pain and mended her emotional scars, just by being there. He wasted no time in finding the man. He asked no questions and said nothing. He walked up to him and broke his arm in one swift move. Ian became a wanted man.

In Jamaica, if someone goes to prison it can be for a long time, no matter how severe or moderate the crime is. If you don't have the money to get yourself out of it, it can be very bad. This was an unexpected twist in Ian's life. Moreover, it had come at a time when he was trying to go straight. When he was a kid he was a thief and now he was a law-abiding citizen, he had skills that allowed him to earn big money. Some people, it is said, are born to be thieves and will always be thieves but Ian didn't believe that; he believed he was a kid born into a poor family but despite this he was still proud of his people and how he had been brought up.

Ian hid from the law once he became a wanted man. They started to hunt him down and he didn't know what to do or where to go, so he called Sarah in England

and said he wanted to go there and join her. The ever faithful Sarah bought a ticket and before Ian knew it he was on a plane to England. As soon as he arrived, he started to look for work. Sarah took him to a few places where labourers were employed from time to time but nothing was available. Finally, he found work as a road sweeper, a job he quickly took to. He met a lot of people and, from what he had seen so far, decided he liked the country. Ian and Sarah were getting on well but they both knew that this was temporary, it wouldn't be forever.

Ian had already rented a little room thanks to someone he had met while he was working. Building work was all Ian was looking for. He knew he could make money, that's what he wanted more than anything. After a while, he managed to get a job with a construction company. The work was easy and the hours were long; he saw less and less of Sarah, but they spoke regularly. Ian started to realise that England can be tough if you can't read and write. There was always a form to fill in or a job description to read. Somehow he would skim over it and carry on. He was making money, had been able to buy a little place and call it home; things were looking good.

About a year later Ian met Elsa, a gorgeous girl from Sweden. He told her she was the love of his life. They ended up getting married and life was going well for them. He started to understand what love was but still couldn't appreciate it. He depended on her for a lot of things and she would help him with anything without a second thought. He worked long hours. Some people paid up and some people didn't, making him wonder just what he was working for but he didn't want to be the guy he used to be. He wanted to live a life completely different to the one he'd lived back home. Sometimes, however, he would be tempted to go back to his old ways and many times when people didn't pay him he would get angry and start to consider his options.

2

Ian worked hard every day. But he thought about a lot of things and realised that his old ways were catching up on him. He started to work longer hours and took more jobs away from home, trying to avoid such feelings.

Elsa and Ian lived in a four-bedroomed detached house in the heart of the City. It was rare to find a house like this in London. When they first saw it Elsa was not amused, she didn't see any potential in its 'décor'. It had broken windows and demolished foundations. But Ian saw the possibility of beauty, to him it was an awesome challenge. The woman offering the property was a retired banker. Ian had done some building work for her in the past and she always recommended him to her friends. She had become quite fond of him too. As she was moving to Croatia she thought she would sell off the properties that were in a state of disrepair as she couldn't rent them anymore. She knew Ian would create a beautiful home for himself and his family so she signed over the deeds in return for an update of the refurbishments.

Ian worked on the house day and night. When it was finished, the house set standards that even the most well-known interior designers and architects couldn't match. The property had a big garden and an electronic driveway. It was worth a small fortune and a huge step up from the one-roomed house Ian was accustomed to. The house was very spacious and even with all five children, including Hope, everyone was still able to find their own quiet area in the house.

When Hope arrived in England she was seven years old and quickly adapted to Western culture. She made lots of friends and was doing exceptionally well in school, a lot better than her classmates. She got on well with Elsa and showed respect both at home and among her peers. She felt nothing was expected of her and relaxed in her new environment, but her morals and self-discipline were impeccable. Strong willed, down to earth and open to all suggestions, Ian could not believe that this was his little girl. He knew with the unconditional love of Elsa, Hope could only continue to blossom.

Ian was still working away from home a lot. While he was away he felt he could work off any pressures that he was burdened with. He was afraid he'd be unable to meet payment deadlines, buy the kids school shoes, support Elsa, feed the babies and, to top it all off, there was a guy who owed him a lot of money. Every time he went to get his money, the guy would keep on telling him stories about his inability to pay him. Ian thought he'd do things the right way so he took the guy to court. Unfortunately, he lost the case. It was bemusing to Ian and in the end he decided he wouldn't go along with the court's decision. It simply hadn't been a just outcome.

One day Ian and the man bumped into each other. When the man saw Ian he gave him a cheeky grin and said, "Hello, how can I help?" Ian wasn't happy. Not only had the court said he had to leave the situation alone, as though he was a liar, this man was now mocking him. So Ian pulled out his Stanley knife and ripped it down the man's inner leg as he walked by, catching his main vein. He watched as the man bled and seeing him die gave Ian a lot of pleasure. He didn't get his money but he was content. It wasn't even about the money in the end, it was the principle of it. The police couldn't prove what had happened or who had committed the murder; to be sure, the cops brought him in first as he was a likely suspect but they didn't have any physical evidence, just a motive. Ian felt good. A kind of good he hadn't felt for a long time. The cops were still seeking evidence to use against Ian but in truth they merely wanted to be seen as doing their job. This was the event that changed Ian's life, more powerful than the birth of his children, more than the connection between him and Elsa, his first love. His ambition had finally been realised.

While he was at home that evening, Ian got himself together and put some things in a small holdall. He always had money put away in the house in case of emergencies. He took it all out and put it on Elsa's dresser. He took out all the bank books and cards, the deeds for the property, the bonds and records of the children's trust funds. Elsa had entered the room after putting the baby to sleep. Even though she was puzzled by the well-organised documentation and the tremendous amount of money sitting on the dresser, she never questioned what Ian did. Sometimes he was a little unorthodox in his thoughts and ways but that was her man and he was her soul mate. He gave her his policy details, accidental death and life insurance and all the indemnity policies. Elsa cried. She knew what this meant. She was losing her man, infact she was never sure, she ever had. With a tear in his eye, Ian leaned over and kissed Elsa, a kiss that spoke a million words. He put Elsa back onto the bed and there they made love, passion exploding through them. Well, to be honest, I just made that bit up. I guess that's what happened; Ian would never go into that type of detail. He once told me, "a man's real work is done at home, if you tell someone how you do it, before you know it they'll be knocking at your front door trying to get a job". Come on now, I wouldn't tell you either, a man's got to have a little privacy.

Anyway, Ian got up the next morning and went to work as usual, worked out his day and left. Ian disappeared into deep suburbia. A few days later his van was found under some railway arches. It was burnt out and it was noticeable that the van had been in a crazy accident before it caught fire, leaving a pile of ashes in the van. This led to one conclusion. Although DNA testing was known in the early eighties, the techniques used in those days were limited and therefore deemed to be unreliable. Trying to identify the body was definitely out of the question. It was the van details that led the police to knock on Elsa's door, and as Elsa had not seen Ian for a few days it was presumed to be his ashes that remained in the van.

Elsa gave the police the details she had prepared in case of such an eventuality. The children were young and missed their dad. Hope was comforted by Elsa's never-failing calm spirit, she became stronger and a pillar of strength for her little brothers and sisters. It wasn't long before life seemed to get back to normal, everyone's support and good wishes came in abundance.

Ian went away to start a different life. This wasn't the first time that Ian had walked away from his family and what he knew but this time it felt different; he had stopped trying to hold back the dreams and bad feelings. He was going to be all he had ever desired. The life he dreamed of when he was a kid, the life of an assassin. Ian was well liked, people respected him. He was a quiet warrior, one that didn't roar before the war. He kept himself to himself and didn't borrow or want from anybody. His family were well mannered and polite. Gloom filled the city the day he was buried. An assassin? No one could believe it. To become an assassin would require great evil, deceit, lack of conscience. That wasn't really Ian, was it?

Ian had 'turned'. It was all about vengeance; good prevailing over evil.

The suburbs were a whole world away from the city. Trees lined the streets, animals roamed the fields. No one would look for Ian here. As he walked through the dusty town, miles away from anywhere, he knew this was the place. He went into a broken down store and found the lady was happy to see someone. She greeted him by welcoming him to Inklingshire. Ian didn't reply, he just looked up and glanced at her. She continued to talk, clearly using Ian as a sound off. Ian approached the counter, where the lady was standing next to the cash register. She remarked that he didn't talk much and wondered if he was okay. "Are you going far? Where are you coming from? Who are you coming to see? Do you need somewhere to stay?" She just didn't stop. Ian put the money on the counter and took his bag. He didn't wait for the change. The lady didn't charge him for the detailed road map he had put in the back of his trousers – not that he wanted to steal it even though he knew he could get away with it. She shouted after him for the change, but as she opened the door to see where he had gone, Ian was nowhere to be found.

Ian found a rickety farmhouse, a few miles from the store. In fact it was the first building he'd seen since he left the store. Admittedly, he didn't walk along the dirty road but the whole area was unchartered territory.

Perfect. The house was fully furnished with clothes in the closet but it was obvious that no one had lived in the patchy old farmhouse for many years. Some food in the cupboards had become rotten years ago. The farmhouse was all on one level, with a hatch to the basement in the cloak room, near the middle of the hallway. The back door was an exact replica of the front – you wouldn't have known which was which. I guess it wouldn't matter as there was no defined path or road to the house. This was a quiet place Ian was unaware of: nothing to see from all corners of your home but hot, dusky silence. He felt slightly disarmed and so he sat and let the silent winds and the turning of the sun guide him. Within days Ian felt in control of himself and his elements, he could tell you the time through his shadow, the weather through his body temperature and the smell of the air. He was at one with the elements. It was time.

Ian set up a PO Box address, 999 HOPE. The collecting office was situated at the back of a supermarket, 25 miles from the house. He already had a phone line but needed a diverter so that the calls couldn't be traced. Some cables and some wires would do it. Ian was the whizz-kid after all. But hardware stores were difficult to find in suburbia and consisted mainly of the usual family stores with food, crisps, Pepsi and so on. Shops with chisels and nails went by the usual motto, 'if we don't have it, we'll order it'. But Ian wanted it now. He was thinking big, maybe too big to start off with. He started with a pile of newspapers and magazines, ranging from local to regional news, old and new. Here he would find stories of the people who had been victimised or betrayed and follow the stories through the news reports. He would collect profiles, character references, background, areas, and addresses. Then he would put all his investigations into organised piles, putting codes onto each one.

Ian called upon the skills of Shadow and Flame. These were his brothers from the ghetto. Many a time, while undergoing the stresses and struggles of trying to survive on his own in Jamaica, Ian would meet these guys on the streets. They would be looking for the same thing as him, a piece of food here, a drink of water there. Ian trusted these guys implicitly and he was sure they were more than up for the job, they were his closest companions. He had brought them over from Jamaica and got them good jobs working on a building site. They felt that Ian was their saviour, someone who had taken them from nothing and made them into something.

While waiting for the guys to arrive, Ian cleaned out the house, making mental notes of areas between doors and windows, creaky floorboards and noting the number of footsteps between each room. He fixed and replaced things throughout the house, removing any unnecessary items and placing them in the barn, just in case the previous owner returned. When he got back to the hallway, he remembered the hatch to the basement. Ian had to cut out the hatch as the edges were soldered together. Whatever was down there, it was not meant to be interrupted. Ian jumped into the room and fell onto a chair and some old dusty suitcases. He coughed through the dust, swiping away cobwebs. Then he felt for the light switch and pulled. As the light flickered into life Ian became more and more aware of what was down there. He was bemused. Destiny, it was all destiny, what else could it be?

When Shadow arrived he was full of dust. He was confused but smiling as he too stopped at the broken-down store. His first questions were "Who is that woman?" and "Where are we?"

Ian quickly jumped in and said, "You sound just like the woman." They smiled and gave each other a touch, shoulder to shoulder, ghetto brother style. Shadow was strong and broad, like an American football player. He could knock you out with one silent punch, standing upright. Not only was he solid, he was empathetic, sensitive, loyal, sensible and true.

Flame was a comedian. When he arrived he was walking like a drunk, he had his shirt out and he was dragging his bag along the ground. He looked at the house as though it was an oasis and saw Ian and Shadow as though they were in his imagination, begging God to get him out of the desert and away from the talking lady who loved a black man. He said that bit with a menacing smile while rubbing his belly. That could only mean one thing, no wonder he was late. Shadow threw a knife at him and like a magnet to metal he straightened up, spun, and caught the knife under his arm. The team was made.

The next morning, Shadow and Flame woke up to a traditional Jamaican breakfast of ackee and salt fish, callalou, bammy, breadfruit, plantain, hard dough bread. It was endless. Their eyes watered at the sight of the food. In all their time in England they'd never felt at home until now. They had always just been passing through. They never intended to stay in England; they wanted to make enough money to go back home and live good with what they had, that was the idea. Like Ian, they didn't have any family back home to support. They were living for themselves. Even though their country treated them badly, they loved it and what it had made of them. Surrounded by good food, good company, warm air; there was lively conversation, no need to talk soft and slow allowing the 'natives' enough time to understand what they were saying to them. What more could they want at that point? Ian had done it again. He had saved their lives, their heritage, their friendship, their memories, without even knowing it. After breakfast, they relaxed on the porch with a glass of cool lemonade. The time was now nearing midday and Ian felt it was time to show the guys just what they were here for.

He walked the guys to the hallway where the cloakroom was situated. He turned and asked his ghetto brothers, "In all the time you've known me, what was the one thing that kept me going, what have I always believed in, what have I always wanted to be?"

Flame raised his hand as though he was in court ready to swear upon the Bible. "Blouse knart," he replied, "afta ya dun mek how much pickney now sah, it must be assassin time, nah mon." He didn't hesitate, he had looked upon Ian as a leader from the day he had met him. He would fight for the food just to give it away. He'd say he was 'feeding the pleading'. Anything Ian did was for the good. Flame was behind his brother all the way. He stepped onto the newly built staircase leading towards the basement.

Shadow, on the other hand, although he knew this was Ian's yearning, saw the right and wrong side of it all, and he was faithful and hopeful. Although life had dealt him some really bad cards, he remained optimistic. He stood for a while and paused for a minute to think. He realised that despite all the bad cards he had received, Ian had helped him to overturn them every time. He was in, but he made it clear he would not kill anyone unless it was to save a life or in self defence. He followed Flame down into the basement with Ian just a few steps behind.

Flame stood on the last step with his jaw wide open. Shadow pushed him forward and bounced him off the step. There was no sound. That was unusual for Flame. As Shadow took the last step, he forgot all about Flame's unusual lack of reaction to his manhandling him. Ian sat a few steps up from the ground and watched his friends marvel at the contents and workmanship there in the basement.

The day Ian fell into the basement, he couldn't believe what he saw. The room was full of tools, computer screens, hard drives, weapons galore, guns, knives, machetes, knuckledusters – and machine guns. I mean real heavy artillery: grenades, hand missiles, poisonous gasses. A lot of it looked like early World War Two weaponry, especially the gas tanks and hand launchers, but they were all in perfect condition.

The first job that came in was from a middle-aged man who called himself John. He remarked that the papers called him this for legal reasons. He spoke in spurts, almost as though he was being pushed along. He stuttered when he said his daughter had been raped and Ian felt his pain immediately. "I want that man dead, I want that man dead, do you understand? I want him dead." His calm demeanour had disappeared and his rage was now showing through. Ian asked him if he knew the man's name or where he could be found but by this time the man was so distraught it was hard to make out what he was saying. Ian only caught the words 'school' and 'cafeteria'. He looked at the note that came with the telephone number; the postmark showed Barclay, a big town 73 miles north of the farmhouse. He put the number into the database to create a search, which took a few minutes. The search showed the billing address and names on the account. It also showed the last numbers dialled, incoming and outgoing. The address showed Barclay as the town, just as the postmark said, the names being Mr and Mrs Mason. Shadow keyed in 'Fountain High School'. In doing so, he found the names of students, staff, the address, funding; everything came up. He shifted through the student list and found a 'Maddy Mason'. The school was also in Barclay and less than two kilometres from the Masons' billing address. It seemed so easy. Could this be the same little girl whose daddy wanted her rapist dead? Ian turned to Shadow who explained that he had been reading the regional newspaper and come across an article about a child who had been raped by the school cook. The town was Barclay and the father's name had been changed to John for legal reasons. He was being held for Actual Bodily Harm for attacking the man both he and the police had suspected of hurting his little girl. Ian looked at Flame, kissed his teeth and went to get the papers. Here he read the news story from the beginning.

Ian was surprised to see the man who had been accused of such a crime and awaiting a court hearing was free to walk the streets. He had been in Barclay for the last two days, watching the suspect. The town was big but it still lacked the amenities that make a town a city. The people were pleasant and non-invasive. Ian didn't make his presence known; he kept out of sight but remained alert. It was evident that the man the crew had now nicknamed 'Dead' was leaving town with his family, just to the cabin. Flame had heard Dead's wife tell their neighbour. They left in the family car followed by Ian, Shadow and Flame.

Shadow called the number. Mr Mason, 'John', answered. He said, "I will ask you one simple question, how do you want it done?" John said, "Just do it and bring me back a souvenir."

They had been on the road for a little over an hour. The sunny blue sky was blocked by the overgrown trees and the heavy evergreens. In the distance they could see Dead's car approaching a broken down cabin, secluded and peaceful. The family got out of the car and one by one took the bags with them into the cabin. It was just after midday before anyone came out. It was Dead holding the barbeque. He walked it a few yards from the side of the cabin then placed it on the ground next to some coal. The little boy followed with a tray of food. Flame announced, "Blouse knart, hot dog, cha, nut a nuton fi we."

Shadow chuckled and rubbed his tummy, Ian kissed his teeth. "Yow a serious ting dis ya knuh bredrin." The guys became silent but couldn't help smiling. After a few hours the children were left fishing on the pier while Dead and his wife went back into the house. Ian felt this was the time. Why wait for night to come? After all, he didn't wait when he raped little Maddy. Shadow, Flame and Ian separated, each of them wearing sunglasses, manoeuvring around the cabin so as not to be seen, giving signals to show where the children were and where Dead and his wife were in the house. As Ian approached the front door he was conscious of where every member of the family was.

He knocked on the door and entered. He was face to face with Dead. Ian asked him his name although he knew it was him from the reports and news broadcasts. Dead stuttered as he gave his name in full. He tried to straighten up and asked, "Who are you, what is this?" His wife started to back up and fell into a chair in the far corner of the room. She said nothing. She was whimpering and shaking.

Ian turned and said to Dead's wife in a cool, almost seductive voice, "I'm sorry but I have to kill your husband, he has committed a terrible crime." He slit his throat there and then with one swift swipe. Ian stepped back leaving Dead to drop to the ground. He stood over him and said, "For Maddy." Then he removed Dead's finger and wrapped it in a handkerchief.

Dead's wife stayed perfectly still, calm, almost relieved. Shadow touched her shoulder and said, "It's over."

She placed her hand on his, gripped it tightly and said, "Thank you." Ian and Shadow walked out of the cabin without looking back. Flame was in the car with the engine running. Ian was feeling good as he made his way to the car, he felt no remorse. He was on a high and wondered where and when the next job would turn up. The ride home was silent.

The next morning, Shadow and Flame woke to find Ian on the veranda trolling through the newspapers. They were sitting down on the day chair. Nothing was said. After a while Ian took the phone and dialled the number of 'John'.

"Hello," said John.

Ian said, "I have it."

John sat down. "Thank you, thank you, err, where should I meet you?" John sounded as though he was back in control of his life.

When Ian came back, he shared out the money; a fifth each for him and the guys, a fifth towards the operations and the rest towards amenities. Everyone thought this was fair. Ian didn't give John a figure, he picked up the bag and made his way home, but even after the divide every man was still honoured by more than a few thousand pounds.

Flame placed his money in his mattress. Shadow held the money in his hand, looking bewildered. He sat for a while until finally Flame nudged him and said, "wharphen star."

After a few seconds Shadow rose from the chair and walked over to Ian. "Yesterday, you were different. As well as I know you, I didn't know that man. It would seem through all the struggles we have come to this… this. It is as though you have…" Here he raised his head as though realisation had struck him. "You have turned. That's it – turned. This is your dream and your will. I am here for you, as long as it is for the good, Turn."

Ian heard Shadow's words but felt the name more. Turn, yes, that described him, he had turned. Even though he had wanted this for a long time it wasn't until now that the nightmarish dreams had stopped, the bad feelings and thoughts had vanished; he felt happy. He believed he was doing good, defending the weak by rectifying the wrongs, but on the other hand he knew he was committing crimes. He had achieved his dream and his two accomplices, Shadow and Flame, ensured it was a good team. Turn was feeling good.

Jobs came through slowly at first, just once a week or so. After a few months, it became a daily occurrence. The influx of calls and notes came in abundance from people requesting their services. Some were from places Turn had never even seen on the road map. They had started a mob that would prevail for years to come.

One of the cases that came through was from a lady with a two-year-old daughter. Case number ninety-three. She said that her daughter was being abused by a local man. She knew he had abused other children but couldn't prove it. After some research, Turn found out that he was a paedophile and on the government's wanted list. He told the 'ninety three' lady that he'd do this one for free. Turn didn't like people like that, he hated them. But ninety-three insisted. That way she'd feel as though she'd really had initiated it, the killing of a man who had physically spoilt her daughter. Turn knew what she was feeling. He remembered the time his daughter was assaulted and what he did when he found the man. He still felt proud of his intentions and actions, and this job would be satisfying. He pressed the button to end the call. He had a heavy heart.

Turn, Flame and Shadow arrived in the city. The lady had given him full details of the local man's whereabouts, where he hung about, the time he left for work, the time he came home, even the roads he walked on. The team didn't have to search for him. In fact, as they drove along one of the roads, they actually saw him. Shadow jumped out of the car to keep track of him although they knew they couldn't lose him given all the information they had on him. The lady had certainly done her homework on him: number ninety-three was serious. Turn liked that.

Shadow followed discreetly. He watched how Dead walked along the side road and how he put his hands in his pockets as he slowly passed the children, greeting each one of them separately. Shadow was beginning to feel disturbed, he felt consumed with rage at every step. From out of the shade came a lady, looking straight at him. She walked past him but said nothing; she just nodded. Shadow felt at ease with his distraction and continued.

Turn and Flame settled into the hideout. The two of them would always found a hideout while they researched the next job. Being on site made surveillance a lot easier.

When Shadow got to the hideout, everything was already set up. He went straight to the computer and switched on the tracker. He felt compelled to watch this man Dead, noting his routes and times. When a job was in progress, Turn hardly slept. The others would be knocked out, but this time Shadow and Turn stayed awake; they were becoming frustrated by the man and his wrongs.

The next morning Dead was up at his usual time, just like clockwork. When he had left his flat he got into the lift and made his way to his car. He had a flat tyre. "Damn!" he shouted, and quickly put on the spare, thinking nothing of it. He got in his car and drove to his first spot. On his way there, he came across roadwork signs. He felt a little disgruntled by the signs and went to his next spot. He stopped to park outside a busy leisure centre. The guys watched him as he spoke with and laughed with the children who were waiting to be picked up. Turn felt sick while Shadow rubbed his chin in annoyance. Flame wasn't feeling the same as the others, he just knew he had read a lot of disturbing things about this man and wanted him dead. It was simple for him. Dead moved from there, slowly circulating the schools and left to eat in the kebab shop, watching the school kids coming in and out. After a while he got up and went back to the leisure centre, where he went in and watched the children play five-a-side football. He stayed there throughout the evening until finally leaving at closing time, slowly making his way back home alone.

The next morning Dead was up at the usual time. After walking down 15 flights of stairs because the lift was unexpectedly out of order, he found three of his tyres split and flat. He was not amused and believed that someone was playing tricks on him. He left the car and walked quickly to his first destination, the library. It was a Saturday and the morning book club had begun. He was a volunteer reader for the toddler group and nothing would stop him from being there. When he had finished reading he helped the children choose their favourite book and two hours later he left and headed for the cinema. He went inside and bought a ticket for the children's world animation film. Dead sat in a row just behind a group of children, offered them his sweets and popcorn, and started a conversation. When the film had finished, Turn emerged from the cinema. A lady was walking out next to him. She looked at him as Shadow, who was on watch in the car, saw them both while they were walking out of the cinema. It was the same lady that had eased him in his time of frustration. Turn had noticed this lady out of the corner of his eye; she hadn't stopped looking at him so he turned to look at her. Usually, people would avert their gaze, but not her. She looked into Turn's eyes and said, "You have set me free." Turn was mesmerised. She was not much taller than five foot, with long dark hair, like a native apache, her eyes as black as midnight. Her beauty was intense and she sang in a calm and dulcet tone. She was amazing. Had she seen what had happened? No, she couldn't have. Turn was careful, he knew where everyone in the room was. Flame was his look out and he never sent any warnings. *You have set me free*. What did she mean by that?

In the cinema the credits were rolling. Turn moved seats, to sit behind Dead. Dead didn't leave like everyone else, he sat and watched the kids as they walked towards the exit. As Turn sat down he noted that Dead's hand was inside his trouser front. He shivered at the thought. The room was empty and still Dead remained in his seat, oblivious to the two spectators. Turn examined his intended victim. His hair was a greasy, mousey blonde, wavering on the top and sides; his neck and ears were hairy and his skin was full of freckles with beads of sweat covering his pores. Turn didn't like this man. Dead's breathing was getting harder and harder, it was clear what he was doing. Turn took his knife and got into position. Meanwhile, Dead had reached his peak. He shuddered in the chair before shooting his head back on the seat, his eyes shut tightly. He was still convulsing. Turn stood over him and launched his knife into his throat. The blood spit like a bullet from a gun, but luckily it missed Turn. He made sure he left Dead in the same position. That is how people should find him. Let the judgements commence upon a man who had violated the precious souls and innocence of so many children.

The crew returned to the hideout where they prepared to make their way home. Turn dialled the lady's home number as they were nearly ready to pack up the cars and go. A little boy answered but before Turn could ask for anyone the lady took the telephone and said, "I knew you would call, I have left it in the empty cupboard in the kitchen. I appreciate you must be going now but thank you for your time and services." The phone went dead. Turn was bemused, he was sure he had heard the voice before. He shouted at Flame to make sure he had emptied the kitchen cupboards. Flame ran through all the cupboards: 'a wha dis'. He came into the room with a travel pack for the way home. It was clearly heavy. He put it down in the middle of the room. All the guys were curious as Flame investigated the bag. Turn told the guys about the conversation he'd just had with the lady. Shadow knew it was the same lady, the one who looked straight at him, the one who came out of the cinema with Turn. It was her. Flame opened the bag and could only see money; the bag was full to the brim with fifty pound notes. "Whata ting." Ninety-three was serious.

Once again the guys returned home and the money was divided into five: a fifth to Flame, a fifth to Shadow, a fifth to Turn, a fifth to the amenities and a fifth to the operations. Money was plentiful and the crew were stronger than ever. They had found a release from the problems of society but most importantly they all believed that what they did was *good*, helping to create harmony in the world.

Turn thought about Elsa. It had been a long time since she'd appeared in his dreams. He wondered how she was coping and how big the children were. He had been away nearly ten years. At first he was very nonchalant about leaving her to pursue his calling but now he was curious about their lives and desires.

It was the last Friday of the month. There was a knock at the door and Elsa knew full well who it was and what they had for her. As usual it was that man. They had both finally come to a compromise and called it 'Man Friday'. It was obvious and funny, so why not? For nearly ten years Elsa had opened the door, said thank you and closed it again. She had asked Man Friday in a few times but he always declined the offer. When Ian passed away Man Friday appeared. In fact it was the first Friday after the funeral. He introduced himself as a Personal Insurance Trust Fund Operator. Elsa didn't know what that was, but accepted it nonetheless. He advised Elsa that she would receive money on the last Friday of every month. This money would be enough to send the children to school and university, as well as maintain the house and allow her to live the life she was accustomed to. The first time Elsa opened the envelope she closed it quickly, went into her room then locked the door. She went to her bathroom, sat in the shower tray and took the envelope out of her jumper. Next, she opened the envelope again. Ian had never left her or the children short, but this was too much. There was enough money in there to buy the house and still buy some cornflakes with the change – and I mean the real stuff, not that corner shop rubbish. Elsa was careful with the money. She paid all the bills in cash and put set amounts away in the children's bank accounts. School, college and university fees were also paid for in cash and when the children needed something it was immediately paid for. Elsa didn't even use her credit cards, she paid them off gradually with the money. She was wise enough to put them away for a just-in-case moment. This Friday Elsa was determined to get Man Friday in the house and have a real conversation with him.

Aaron, aka Man Friday, was a twenty-something guy with astronomical ambitions; you know, the kind that rarely gets anywhere. Well, he saw an ad in the paper one day asking for help with deliveries. The advertisement had a PO Box address for replies and he made up his mind to apply for it. He wasn't really looking for a job but he told his parents he was trying to get one as he was well past the age of adolescence. He was surprised when he got a call from Shadow to say his application had been successful. Of course, the crew carried out a thorough check on Aaron; his date of birth, address, family ties and any other links that seemed relevant, just to make sure he was legit.

Judging by his college reports, it was evident that Aaron was a young man with a lively imagination; he was bright and always creating new gadgets. That was all he was really interested in, he barely earned pass grades in his other subjects but he was awarded the academic national prize for his inventions, many of which were used in the classrooms. Aaron was polite and courteous, even though he had never met the guys. He always said thank you on the phone and showed great respect. This may have been due to the fact that within five years he was able to buy his own house in the suburbs, pay his parents' bills and create his own work studio. He was adamant that he would eventually make an invention that would be used by everyone in the world and this job allowed him to do that. Aaron was discreet and easy, no one asked where he got his money from, they believed it was from a silent donor or partner. Aaron was more than cool with this arrangement. Shadow had explained to him that there would be no contact and that he only had to make one delivery a month. Obviously he was sceptical but he was assured that this was not a drug enterprise and he would only be carrying the same set amount of money. The key was to be discreet and answer no questions, it was simply a delivery. He was reminded that he would be followed to ensure the package was delivered and received. Aaron would pick up the money on a Thursday evening from different locations, take out his wages and deliver the rest of the money to Elsa on Friday morning at 10.30, rain or shine.

One Thursday at 6pm, Aaron answered the phone expecting to hear Shadow's voice. Instead he heard a voice he did not recognise. Although the voice was calm yet commanding, Aaron stood his ground and said nothing. He only wanted to hear Shadow's voice; that was the agreement. Turn, even though he was slightly pissed off about it, was quite happy that this boy who he had picked could be this loyal to someone he had never met before. He had definitely become quite fond of Shadow and gleamed with appreciation of his telephone friend. After Shadow had introduced Turn as his manager, Aaron sat and listened attentively. Turn suggested to Aaron that he and Elsa must be good friends by now, but Aaron rejected that suggestion. He told Turn that he made no effort to be friendly with the lady he delivered the money to and knew little about her. He admitted that she had invited him in a few times, but he always declined. Turn asked if she was curious or asked any questions. Aaron replied that he always told Elsa the same thing, he was a Personal Insurance Trust Fund Operator who had been given the task of delivering the policy pay out which Ms Elsa was due to receive, following the death of her husband Ian. This was thanks to a personal policy created by Ian. It was paid in cash and there was no reference to any tax liability. Turn asked if he had seen any of the children. Aaron had only seen a few of them as they passed him coming in or out and he had heard them calling for their mum but he didn't who was who or even if they were the children he was referring to. After a long talk, Aaron went to pick up the package. He had a new task, or so it seemed. He was going to investigate without arousing suspicions. He felt like a spy, 007, and chuckled. There was no way he could have handled all those women at one time anyway.

To Elsa's surprise, Man Friday didn't hesitate. He came in and sat down, relaxed but still conservative. His back was straight, clothes neat, words pronounced correctly and to the point. He was careful as to how he answered Elsa's questions, even though he didn't really know anything about the situation. As far as he was aware he had been asked to deliver the money to her and he was getting paid to do it so why not?

Elsa offered Man Friday a cup of tea. He accepted graciously. While she was out of the room Aaron looked at the pictures on the wall and along the mantle piece. It was full. He smiled at some of them. The family looked extremely close. There was one picture of a man, slightly out of focus, enough to distort his image but not enough to distort the picture. It resembled a guardian figure with five children surrounding him. This particular photo stood out from the rest, it seemed to tell a thousand stories all ending happily ever after. Aaron wondered if this was Shadow's boss but before he could let his imagination run away with him he noticed the next image, which stood prominently in the middle. It was a reflective frame which held a mirror image of a man's face. The outline and curves of his facial features could be seen, it was dominant but not imposing. He could see his full reflection; it was fascinating, calm and comforting and made him feel like he wasn't alone. It was beautifully done.

Elsa entered the room and watched as Aaron looked at the picture. After a while Elsa said, "It still catches me sometimes as well." Aaron turned and asked who it was. Elsa lowered the tray onto the coffee table and slowly looked up to face Aaron. "That is Ian, he passed away some time ago, he's why I see you every last Friday of the month, he is the father of my children." Elsa sat down. "It was a long time ago, but it feels like he is still with me. The children have all grown up now, they only remember little things about him but they have flourished in his memory and are wonderful people." She smiled. Aaron sat down and picked up a mug from the tray and allowed Elsa to express herself. It was obvious she was still hurting from the loss but her strength was urging her on to new things. She pulled down the picture of the five children with Ian and named them all, giving a little story about each one. They were all quite young in the picture, but it was easy to tell who was who from the other pictures of them as they had grown older. Ian junior and Hope were the spitting image of Ian. They were the oldest, the other three children were just like Elsa. Even Jason, the youngest son, had all the features of Elsa and had a broad build. "He may look like me," said Elsa, "but he has the body of an ox. He is very boisterous, he fights a lot, he winds up his sisters, and he is just like Ian. His inner strength is almost unbreakable. He is stubborn at times and holds his ground. But he knows right from wrong and never disrespects anyone; he and Hope are very close." Then Elsa began to tidy up a little. She fixed the cushions and replaced the picture back on the mantelpiece before walking over to the table next to the armchair. There was a picture there which featured someone Aaron hadn't seen in the other photos. "This is Greg, he's my fiancé, do you think it's too soon for me to get married again?"

Aaron felt a little caught out. "From what I have seen and heard here today from you, Elsa, you are clearly ready, you have nourished and brought up your children single-handedly and they respect you for keeping the memory of their father alive. Even with Greg in your life, I'm sure you're not a lady to rush important decisions. Whichever decision you make it won't be wrong, Ian is still with you in mind and spirit. He would let you know if it was wrong for you in anyway." Aaron stood up and looked at the time before placing his mug on the tray. He reached out to shake Elsa's hand. "I will let you get on with your day, thank you for the tea and I'll see you next month," he said with a smile. Elsa smiled back and assured him that there would always be a cup of tea waiting for him.

"Thank you for sharing some time with me," she said as he walked up the path and out the gate. Elsa closed the door. It had been a refreshing change talking to Aaron.

3

The crew had been on top of their game for nearly six years. They were becoming inundated with requests for the use of their services and were filthy rich. Turn had bought a huge house on the hill, a house that afforded a view of miles and even counties. It was a long way from the road and at least six miles up along a dirt track. It sat next to an old cemetery, which led some people to say it was haunted, while others just couldn't get up the slip road that led to it, leaving it overgrown and broken down. They restored the farmhouse and made sure all the equipment that was left in the basement was in good condition, good enough for domestic use. Turn didn't want anybody trying to follow their tracks, so anything dangerous was removed and they always made sure to wash and wipe all the surfaces, any one of which may have had traces of who used to reside at the house. The basement trapdoor was sealed and the guys left. According to the auctioneer the mansion had been empty for roughly 15 years and Turn was the only one who had made a bid for it. "Clearly too much work for Englishmen," joked Flame.

The mansion had secret doors, secret passages, and secret tunnels, which led to the bottom of the hill or near the lake. It was easy to get lost in there and the guys were ready and willing to get stuck into some plastering. They hadn't done any building work since moving to the farmhouse and thoroughly enjoyed getting dirty and seeing the end result. "Aghh, the fruits of labour," said Shadow.

The killing commenced. "Breaktime done!" shouted Flame. He had just walked in with the mail from the PO Box address. Under his arm he had all the newspapers rolled into one and was struggling with the door key. He tried to hold all the requests in both hands but as he stepped in he stumbled and fell down the three steps leading down to the open lounge area. Turn and Shadow tried to contain themselves but it wasn't easy. With the amount of mail that Flame had just come in with, they knew there was no time to chuckle, people needed them now.

There were cases from all kinds of people. Some seemed to be linked somehow; addresses, names, descriptions. After some research, if they were sure these requests were about one person they would pile into the car and eliminate the wanted person immediately. If one person could cause so much havoc that more than one person was calling them for their services, the crew felt it to be a 'jump on' situation. Why hang around? One example was 23 letters from one town. A local quiet neighbourhood was being burgled by one man but no one could catch him. He would take anything valuable as well as anything that would enable someone else to use the victim's identity. He burgled one street in two nights, with some people not even realising they'd been burgled until they were looking for a piece of jewellery or their passports. The guys were waiting for him as he came out of a fifth floor apartment via the window. He carefully manoeuvred down the wall – he was a pro at wall climbing – catching ledges and never losing his grip. It was actually really good to watch. As he landed, Flame tripped him up and Shadow stood on his neck. Shadow was a size fourteen so he left quite an impression. Turn knelt beside him and dusted the excess foliage from his shoulders. "What's your name?" he said. But it was a little difficult trying to talk with a size fourteen in his neck.

Eventually he managed to say, "Michael Philips."

The guys grinned as the thief struggled beneath Shadow's big magnum boots. Then Turn scraped up some dirt from under the bushes and rubbed it over Michael's eyes, leaving him unable to see properly. They pulled him into the car and drove him to his house before taking him in and sitting him down. "Michael, you is a teef, and you have to feel the consequences for that," said Turn, "where are the goods?"

Michael, not realising that they had brought him home said, "It's all in the walk-in wardrobe behind the bathroom wall, but I have to make a call first to make sure my flatmate's not in before you collect it, we can go halves if you let me go."

Turn slapped Michael round the face, so hard his neck cricked and he fell to the floor. He knew he was at home. "How did you know where I – "

Before he could finish, Turn grabbed him by the throat and glared at him, furious at the man's proposal as Flame entered the room with bundles of goodies. He asked Michael if that was it, whether there would be any more he hadn't told them about, whether the consequences would be worse. Michael cried as he pointed out different places in the bedsit where he had stashed the rest of the things. When the crew were satisfied, they asked Michael if he was hungry. Through his tears, he said that he was so Flame walked him over to the kitchen area and let him do himself a sandwich. He filled it with all types of things from the fridge then sat and ate the sandwich like a little kid who hadn't eaten for days. Anxious as to what would happen next, he touched his face; it was swollen from the slap he'd received. Tears rolled down his face and he was certain it was judgement time for him. He finished his sandwich and put the plate into the sink. Flame and Turn escorted him back to the table and sat him in the chair then stood one on either side of their victim. Turn approached the table with a towel in his hand that he had folded neatly. He sat down and told Michael to raise his arms off the table then neatly placed the towel in front of him before

49

gently replacing them. Turn sat across the table and spoke softly to Michael. "Tonight I'm going to help you, I'm going to cure you of your dirty habit, would you like that?"

"I have learnt something tonight, sir, I truly want to stop doing what I do." Michael shivered.

Turn started to tut. "If only I could believe that, you have already been in prison twice for the same thing and here we are again. I think the police are tired of you, which is why I am here, it won't take long and you'll remember forever that what you are doing is wrong." As Turn spoke he placed small sharp blades in between his fingers. "Are you ready, Michael?" Before he could reply Turn had gripped his wrists, thrust the blades in, severing tendons and the small capillaries. The pain was so intense Michael couldn't scream. He was in another world. The blood seeped out onto the towel. However, the main vein was not touched and remained intact and after a while the blood slowed down.

"Michael you will never teef again, you're cured, you will sleep for a long time while your body recuperates. When you wake up you will not be able to use your hands, that is your punishment, and your collection will be returned to their rightful owners." They cleaned up the house, removing all traces of themselves, and left. They left the bags of stolen things at the local police station. After a few weeks the crew got a note from one of the elderly residents that had been burgled saying that Michael had unfortunately suffered a terrible fate, he had lost the use of both his hands and she wouldn't be needing their services anymore. The guys chuckled, they had already received payment from the others. The police notified all the residents who had reported being burgled that they had found their belongings.

Had they taken the law into their own hands? Punishing and killing people for their bad deeds; didn't this make *them* bad as well? Turn didn't care. He remembered all the times he had tried to go straight and live right. No matter what he did there was always something against him and it was always bigger than him. He couldn't read, but so what? Was that why he was always the underdog? His childhood was nothing to speak of; hungry, no clothes, fighting, left by his parents. What kind of life was that? He had killed a man because he had stolen his money and he felt he couldn't feed his family. The police didn't have any other suspects, just him, they were going to get him no matter what he said or what they found. Either way, he was feeling good about himself and was not about to change the way things were running. He and his two ghetto brothers were on top and in charge, they were needed and they had never felt that before. He had become a killer while making a lot of people happy and secure. He had also made other people sad. He didn't pay those people much thought as he wanted to become an assassin and that was that.

Turn woke up one morning with a strong urge to learn something new. He went downstairs, fully dressed, and with his bag over his shoulder. He entered the kitchen and poured a small glass of orange juice while the others were engrossed in newspapers and the news updates as usual. Turn finished his juice and picked up his bag. He spoke up. "I'm going away for a while, I'll be home after I have completed my challenge." The guys asked him where he was going but, as he explained, he wasn't really sure himself. "A place far, far away. Take care of yourselves and each other." They said their goodbyes and he left.

It took Turn nearly two weeks to reach his destination in Tibet. Here were the deepest forests, the steepest hills, the meanest elements. But this just made Turn even more determined to reach the top. His dedication and persistence proved to be great attributes to his learning. He was welcomed, they sensed no harm from him, he was pure in heart and they invited him into their home. While he sheltered with the monks he learnt how to slow down his heartbeat, even while moving, and how to make his heartbeat stop completely while he was lying motionless. He could easily be passed as being dead. He learnt about peace, calm and relaxation, reaching a point where pain was just an illusion. Turn had become the ultimate machine. He didn't feel pain and he didn't know how to show remorse. He had been trained in the finest of martial arts, making his hands and feet become weapons, using his entire body – including his mind – as a weapon. After two-and-a-half years of continuous study, he was filled with knowledge;

to understand food and what life meant was a huge investment for any being. Turn had become a master. He could use any weapon given to him: knives, guns, swords, sticks and chains. He demonstrated his skill and agility by putting a large wild tiger to sleep using a match stick. His strength increased and he could break a man's neck with one hand. He could adapt to any environment like a chameleon. He was more powerful than ever. An assassin? You bet he was. He almost scared himself. It was time to go home to see what the guys were up to.

After getting off the plane Turn got into a taxi. When he reached town he asked the driver to stop. He pulled out his bag and gave the driver enough for the journey and a considerable tip. Turn had been away for some time and wanted to walk home to soak in the atmosphere. He wanted to feel the vibes surround him and see what was new. As he weaved in and out of the streets he heard someone screaming, it was coming from the top of a small one-way alley. In the night light he could see a small figure getting pushed around and hit by sticks. As Turn approached he saw a small boy. He looked about twelve years old and he was getting beaten up by three thugs. Turn walked into the middle of the group and asked them what was happening. The thugs weren't happy about the interruption and told Turn in no uncertain terms to make himself scarce.

When they saw that Turn wasn't leaving they became violent and set upon him. He didn't flicker. He resisted them and using his awesome power made light of the fact he was outnumbered. Turn changed direction. The thugs looked at each other and before they knew it he had knocked out one one of them with a well-aimed kick. He displaced the kneecap of another with his knuckle. The third man dropped his stick and started to back away with his mouth open. The little boy lay crying, curled up against the wall. Turn told him not to move. Then he walked towards the third thug and asked him why he would pick on someone smaller than him, why he and his friends would gang up on someone so defenceless. The thug spat out his excuses at an incredible rate. His back hit the wall and Turn squeezed his hand into his belly. He was quickly silenced. He tried to shout out but it made the pain worse. Turn dropped him and he fell to the floor. He had bruised the muscles in the thug's belly, leaving him cramped and unable to move.

Turn walked back to the little boy, and sat him upright. The boy was holding his arm. "What's wrong?" he asked, but he quickly realised they had broken the boy's arm. He took him to the emergency room of a nearby hospital where a doctor examined him. It was a straight break so there was no need for an operation, just a cast. They waited in the family room until the plaster technician came for him. While they were waiting, Turn asked the boy his name.

"My name is Hacker."

"Hacker? Is that your real name?" asked Turn.

"No, I was given that name by one of my foster brothers, there's no computer system that I can't get into, my brain is like a computer."

"So…you're talented?" He paused. "Foster brothers…mmm…what happened to your parents?"

Hacker bowed his head. "My mum died giving birth to me. I never knew my father, I don't even know who he is. I was adopted by the nurse that delivered me but that didn't last long. I was put up for adoption at two because her husband didn't want to raise another man's baby. That's understandable."

"Is it?" said Turn.

Hacker continued. "She was nice and I received lots of letters and home-baked biscuits from her while I was in care, that's if they remembered to forward it to the right address." Hacker looked up. "I'm seventeen now, well past the cute adoption age and just past the age where no one gives a fuck. I've been in 32 foster homes and it felt like every week I was moving home, returning to previous ones, just like a rotating circle."

Turn walked around the waiting area, he could hear what Hacker was saying and it all made sense except for one thing. "Why did you keep moving homes, why didn't they want you there?"

Hacker began to smile. "Well, I would pull things apart to make other things; TV sets and toasters and if someone really got on my nerves I would pull the elements from their radios and put them back together so that when they turned it on it would blow up in their face. Nothing major, just a lot of black smoke. It was real cool until they realised it was me then I got the blame for everything after that, even breaking the toilet roll holder. What would I be doing with that? I'm a sophisticated electronic electrician...toilet roll holder? Please!"

Turn was amused by Hacker's story. He was a good kid but just didn't have anything constructive to do with his time. It was becoming a long night. Turn decided to take Hacker home as he had plenty of room and this boy had lots of potential. During the long walk home, Hacker mentioned that his arm was hurting and that he was feeling drowsy from the effects of the painkillers. His flat, casual canvas shoes were worn out all along the sole. His jacket didn't close and he had to keep holding up his torn trousers because the thugs had taken off his tie-up piece of cord to whip him with. But Hacker didn't grumble about it and Turn admired him for that. The young lad was just glad to be going home somewhere. They had been walking for nearly an hour and a half, on and off, and Hacker was almost lost. He knew he had left the city limits but wasn't sure which way they were going. He was a little apprehensive when he worked out it was a graveyard at the top of the hill but when they eventually levelled out he saw a house that was so huge he thought he was watching TV. He looked over and smiled at Turn. He didn't want to show his excitement, just in case Turn changed his mind. He knew Turn was a serious man and he didn't want to ruin his chances of having someone to look up to.

Turn opened the door. As he did so Flame and Shadow jumped on him from the back. The parameter warning went off when Turn and Hacker came off the dirt track and started walking up the hill. The guys were happy to see him. They greeted and hugged him for a long time then began to speak using their homeland slang. This left Hacker a little bewildered but he was happy at the sight of grown men truly happy just to see each other. They had entered the house and were still welcoming Turn home. Hacker was left outside looking in from the doorway. After a few minutes Shadow asked, "So whose ya fren?"

Turn looked over his shoulder to see that Hacker wasn't there. He went back to the door to find him leaning on one of the pillars. Turn stepped out and said, "What's up?"

Hacker seemed lost. "I had a look inside from the doorway. It's great…no…it's awesome! No! No! No! It's ridiculously wicked, why on earth would you let me stay with you? You guys are obviously rich and don't need a low life to babysit."

Turn looked at Hacker and bowed, holding his arm out to show him the way in. "After you, young man," he said. Hacker stepped in sideways, making sure he didn't mess up the floor with his dirty shoes. Hacker just couldn't believe what he'd stumbled upon that day. Someone was certainly looking after him. Turn introduced him to the guys and explained to them just what Hacker meant. After a light snack and some juice, Turn showed Hacker where he would be sleeping for the night. He told him not to get too comfortable as his room wouldn't be ready for him the next day. Hacker wasn't bothered. The room he was staying in that night was better than anything he could have imagined; clean and cosy, he felt like a baby again wrapped up tightly in a blanket. No fears and nothing to worry about. He dropped onto the bed and as soon as his head hit the pillow he was out. He didn't even manage to take off his shoes. Turn switched off the light and closed the door gently behind him.

Turn went into the operations room where Shadow and Flame were sat watching the screens and monitoring the next target on the list. "Brothers, I was reading the papers on the way back from China, I can see you guys have been taking care of business, lots of things have been happening, let me in on what's new." While Turn was away, Shadow and Flame had continued with the project as if Turn was still with them. They had stepped up the game by removing targets that police had recorded as 'can't find', but they did and they were all worthy cases. Their killings were like a chain reaction – every morning someone had died. People that wouldn't be missed, drug dealers, paedophiles, con artists, rapists, all were wanted on the police list. This was a bonus for the guys; it was like a race to see who could deal with the matter first, but there was never any real contest when they were on the case.

Turn felt good. He was back at home with his brothers. They had held the fort and done so with honour. His trip had revived him. He felt reborn.

4

Noon was approaching fast. The guys were up and in the operations room looking through some reports. Flame went to get Hacker. "Marning, Marning, young bwoy. Marning." Hacker woke up with a smile on his face. Flame liked that, he couldn't take anything too miserable. Flame went into the kitchen and started to prepare Hacker a light lunch, bearing in mind he was asleep when breakfast was up for grabs. Shadow had left a clean t-shirt and some jogging bottoms at the end of Hacker's bed, with a towel and some toiletries. When Hacker emerged from his room he was a clean, sweet-smelling individual, something with which he was wholly unfamiliar. As he came downstairs Flame was just coming out of the kitchen. He looked at Hacker and started to laugh.

"Boy, you're gonna need a lot more than what I made ya to fill them clothes." Shadow had left his own clothes out for Hacker and being the tall, broad-shouldered man he was, the clothes had swallowed Hacker whole and he was still hungry. The elastic in the waist was not enough to hold them so he had to draw the string as tightly as possible. The length of the bottoms made them double as feet warmers while the t-shirt was ridiculous; it was so huge it looked like an over gown. It was a short sleeve and the edges still swam around his wrists. Crazy. Hacker sat down and ate his lunch of salmon and roasted plantain. He ate slowly as it was so good he didn't want it to end. Flame brought out a glass of orange juice and told Hacker to follow the staircase at the back of the kitchen to the operations room.

Thirty minutes later, Hacker knocked on the operations room door. He heard voices telling him to come in. He opened the door and was greeted by huge grins; it was obvious Flame had told the guys and everyone had laughed it out already. He walked down the steps and walked over to Turn. "This room is great, what do you guys do in here? I could think of a million things to do with all this stuff." Shadow stood abruptly, stopping Hacker in his tracks. He rolled his chair over to him and made him sit down.

Turn broke the silence. "Hacker, from now on you are going to be our 'Eyes in the Sky'. We are going to give you a job, one that pays good money, one that you will enjoy. You're going to be our navigator, our satellite navigator in the sky. You will track and find. You will produce profiles and reports collaborated using the projects and files of any relevant agency. Do you accept?"

"Eyes in the Sky is here to stay!" The guys chuckled and slapped hands.

"Welcome to the family, bwoy, welcome." Shadow showed Hacker around the operations room and asked him if there was any other equipment he felt he might need. He looked at Shadow. He really wanted to know what it was all about, who he would be finding, why he was to look for them, profiles and projects, other agencies, all sorts of things. Unfortunately, he didn't know how to ask. The guys had been so good to him and he didn't want them to feel he didn't appreciate it.

"I'll just need some computers, I guess." Shadow caught on to Hacker's hesitant caution and decided to take him out for a drive. Turn was cool with this. Shadow was very diplomatic, gentle and able to speak on all levels. In any case, Turn had things to do. He had to sort out Hacker's room and get him the computers he wanted.

Shadow was very open with Hacker. He explained how they met, how long they'd been in the country, their ups and downs. He told him about Inklingshire and the farmhouse, the mansion next to the cemetery and Turn's trip to China. Hacker was a down-to-earth type of guy and understood what Shadow was saying to him. He thought about their reasons and felt what they did to be a worthwhile cause as he too had been raised in difficult circumstances. He didn't ask much, he didn't need to. Shadow had erased all his doubts and fears about the type of people the crew were. He felt honoured to be a part of an organisation that took action for the undeserving victims. Everyone involved had been demoralised or left to rot in some way by various people or as a result of unfortunate circumstances. It was only natural for him to follow the same path.

It was dark when Shadow and Hacker returned home. They unloaded the truck. It was jam packed with groceries, components and other odd bits. Hacker had already thought of things to make that would help the crew on their missions. Turn raised an eyebrow when he saw three kinds of toaster enter the back suite of the operations room. "What?" said Hacker. "Different brands use different elements." Turn said nothing. He had faith in Hacker and knew he would be a valuable asset to the team.

The guys sat down for dinner. Hacker wasn't hungry as he and Shadow had eaten while they were out. Even so, it didn't stop Shadow from sitting down and telling Flame to, "hurry up and come with the food, yah, man."

Hacker got up and said, "If it's all right with you guys I'd like to have a look around my new home. I swear I won't touch anything or go into your rooms, is it okay?"

"Of course it is, feel free," said Turn who had his head in the newspaper, "but go check out your room first, it's the fourth door as you enter the hallway on the left upstairs."

"Where?" Hacker was baffled.

"Go fish," said Shadow.

Hacker was excited. He felt like a seven year old in a big toy store. After a few misses, Hacker opened what he knew had to be the door. It had to be, it had a palm print verifier on the door knob with a red and green light indicator. "Class," he said. As Hacker pushed open the door wider he swallowed; the room was huge, he couldn't believe it. He entered the room slowly and took it all in. He walked over to the window and looked through the blinds. The skyline surrounded him, he'd died and gone to heaven. He walked to the left where there was an opening into another room. It was a bathroom, which reminded him of the fact he hadn't had a bath for nearly eight years and now within the space of twenty-four hours, he hadn't only had a bath but had now been given his *own* bath. His eyes welled up as he continued to walk through the room into what was an open walk-in wardrobe. It was filled with t-shirts, jeans, socks, underwear, jumpers, and jackets. Hacker felt a cramp in his stomach, like a swarm of butterflies had taken over. He couldn't believe it – the wardrobe led back to his bedroom. By this time he had created a waterfall of tears. Hacker had never asked for anything in his life, and to be given this was as if he was allowed to start life all over again. He felt truly blessed to have ever met Turn in the alley. Hacker sat on his bed gently trying not to mess up the spread. He saw the remotes on the bedside table and the TV, the *huge* TV, hooked up to a VCR and a DVD. They were rare in England, not many people had them yet. A satellite network and surround system too. It was too much. But there was much more. Attached to this was a powerful music system, the latest separates from Kenwood. He didn't know what to do with himself. He decided to programme in the channels and set the equaliser to his taste along with the date and times. There was one remote he hadn't touched. Although it looked like the others, it didn't share the same uses as them. He took the remote and aimed it at the TV. Then he noticed a piece of the wall next to the TV move slightly. He pressed the button again – nothing happened. He walked over to the wall. Next to the window he saw three small black boxes. The top one opened the blinds while the bottom one lowered them. He pressed the middle and got nothing. He put his thumb on it and the wall slid open. "Umm, thumb print verifier." The room was open, very minimal, nothing on the floor and chrome fittings throughout. In the middle of the room stood a computer table and one chair. On the table were two 14-inch flat computer screens in between two 17-inch computer screens. These were attached to hard drives, servers, and Wyse boxes including fax and printer outlets. He sat at the desk and touched the keyboard and the screens lit up. 'EYES IN THE SKY' was written on each screen. "Wow!" It was also written on the mega-sized screen attached to the wall. He swivelled in his chair and noticed a fireman's pole in the corner of the room with a small circular staircase surrounding it. He knew which option he was going to take, even with his arm in plaster: when he got to the bottom, he would drop onto the padding. He laughed out loud and the guys joined him, he was back in the operations room.

The crew had hooked up one of the greatest computer networks ever, and with Hacker's skills they could hack into any file. Hacker was able to get into FBI, MI5, MI6, or government issues. He could hear a bird whistle in China, line up the satellites to see it before you could tell which species it was; there was nothing he couldn't find, read or do using a computer. It was a gift. He certainly wasn't lying when he said his brain was like a computer.

After a couple of weeks Hacker was able to take the long drive to collect the mail all by himself. It was on this drive that Hacker knew he was really a member of the family, welcomed and trusted. Flame had put him under his wing. When they went shopping he would say, "Now you can pick the best yam in the shop, you are destined to be a ghetto brother." Hacker had finally found what he was looking for and he wouldn't do anything to ruin it.

When Hacker returned home Turn was in the open living room. Shadow and Flame had gone out to set up some cameras. Turn looked through the mail, opening a few at a time. Hacker sat back in the chair, he saw no better opportunity than now.

"Why do they call you Turn?"

Turn stopped and placed the mail in his lap. "Turn defines what my life did to me. No matter how many times I tried to twist it back, something, someone, always made it bad. After the first job, Shadow told me that he did not recognise me. When we were younger I would fight for food and give it to them, or try to keep the peace because it just wasn't worth the arms house, everything I did to allow me to step up out of the grime to live straight and right was pushed back in my face. I was beaten, abused, threatened and accused. When I made a home it was taken or I was thrown out like the rubbish. I met some good people along the way but by then I had gone too far. Shadow said I had turned and so that's where my name came from."

Hacker wasn't quite satisfied with the answer, he was happy Turn had opened up and told him but what he really wanted out of it was how they had got here, to the mansion, to the operations room, why?

"So you're wondering how we got here?"

"Well yes, yes I am, young man," said Hacker trying to sound like Flame.

Turn grinned. "For as long as I can remember, young man, I have always wanted to be an assassin. I dreamed so much about it. I would wake up thinking I'd heard someone coming to get me and dodge behind the dresser or the door. Sometimes I would end up beneath the bed. After a few minutes I would snap out of it with sweat on my forehead and cramp in my fingers from thinking I was holding a gun or gripping a stick. I never wanted to be anything else. I have always been the bad one so why not? The minute something occurred I would be thinking about how I'd kill that person, it made me feel better knowing that they would be feeling pain as a punishment for their crime. So after a while my brothers and I came here to this little farmhouse, set up a PO Box address and there you have it. I now work for the victims by upholding their requests. It's a job, I help the innocent and I am an assassin."

"We really are ghetto brothers," said Hacker.

"You wouldn't be here otherwise," Turn replied as he went back to the mail on his lap. "Open some letters, have a look at what these people are going through, try to feel what they're feeling, it will help you understand why remorse is not an issue in this job."

The crew were hooked up to the most powerful satellite system government branded. They listened to police scanners and watched different cameras on the multi-screen hanging on the wall. What's more, there was nothing happening on the streets that they didn't know about. They would seek and find the most wanted criminals out there; drug addicts, for instance, both buyers and sellers. They heard about and read reports of criminals that couldn't be found and laughed as they watched the 'missing person' walking towards a corner shop in the middle of the day. After a couple of years, the police would find that same person dead. It took them a long time to recognise that there was actually somebody out there doing this, it wasn't pure coincidence. Finally, a manhunt was organised but as they didn't know who or what they were looking for, it was deemed a worthless task as well as a waste of time and manpower.

5

Aaron had made a point of writing a detailed report every time he saw Elsa – dates and times, etc. He didn't always take up her invitation, but on the few occasions he did he always felt blessed. Her home was so warm and inviting, her company was never intrusive and she was polite and welcoming. Aaron didn't really have any friends and rarely left his home for anything other than work or his parents. Elsa was a breath of fresh air to him.

In his last report he noted that Hope was graduating at the end of the month. School had finished and she had been accepted into her chosen university. He put the address, date and time of the graduation. Even though he didn't know Shadow's boss he was sure he would appreciate this information. He was right. His thank you call said it all. Aaron felt like a school kid who'd just got an A in his worst subject.

Turn couldn't believe time had gone by without a trace. He pondered on the news from the report. In fact he almost looked forward to receiving them but he wasn't going to let Aaron know that.

Hope was graduating. It was a miracle that she had even been born, let alone alive here in England and now graduating. When Turn had left Jamaica to come to England Hope was nearly six years old. He had left her with her mother Clarisa. As far as Turn was concerned they were in good health and living comfortably; he believed that with the money he was sending weekly and the stable home at the outhouse Cyril and Beverley had provided, things were good for them. When he called, things always sounded okay. Then he received a letter saying that Frank was a man of bad magic. His rituals involved taking pieces from the souls of people while blessing them with their strongest desires. Those who were greedy and kept going back were eventually owned by a darker power, it was evil. It turned out that Hope was born through the wants and desires of Clarisa, who was now owned by Frank. The time was coming for her to give up her first born to Frank and she had refused, stating that her baby was the child of God. Frank didn't like this and put a spell on Clarisa to bring the child. When Beverley noticed the change in Clarisa, she knew she had to contact Turn. Turn was able to get forged documents and return to Jamaica. His sole mission was to save Hope and make sure the magic didn't follow her. Cyril picked him up from the airport and on the journey back he filled him in.

Turn was the first to see Clarisa. She was out of her

mind, rocking and stabbing herself with the fork. Hope was in the corner of the room crying and leaning against the wall, deteriorating, unable to eat or speak. Out of fear of her mother and her fate, she stood in her own excretions, wrapped in nothing but a blanket that he had left her when he was going. Clarisa looked up. She looked terrible, something definitely had her, her eyes were sunken and her skin was rotting away. She dropped to the floor on her hands and knees and begged Turn for mercy, for forgiveness. He didn't know why she was asking him, what could he do? Hope turned around slowly when she heard her mother begging. When she saw her father, she stood strong and wiped the tears from her face. She walked up to her father and stood beside him, his strength vitalising her and making things seem fine. She put her things together and whatever was to happen her dad was not leaving without her this time. Their relationship was one of wonderment, a bond untamed through time, absence or circumstance.

Turn picked up Hope and took her out of the house. He was nearly at the car when he felt something surrounding him. It was not visible but it was strong, it was trying to pull Hope out of his arms but she held on tightly. Clarisa ran outside into a raging wind, holding a machete. She ran straight towards them. Turn held Hope even more tightly and tried to shield her. The wind turned to rain, thunder and sleet as hot as coal was falling to the ground. Clarisa swung with all her might, the machete was heading for Hope. Turn raised his hand to take the hit but the machete glided off Turn, swung past him and Hope, and removed Clarisa's leg. She saw it but she didn't feel it. She was possessed. Turn looked at her as she balanced on one leg, she was breathing heavily and wouldn't let go of the machete. She was motionless. After a few moments she collapsed to the ground, holding her leg, and started screaming.

Beverley ran to her and rocked her in her arms as she prayed. "I am sorry." She looked up. "Take me, I am the one you want, a life for a life, that's all that was asked of me. Not even you can fight a heart as pure as my saviour." With that she held the machete in the sky and plunged it into her chest. Screams filled the air, gusts of wind lifted the dirt off the ground and rocked the cars; the sleet turned to ice and Clarisa's body was suspended in mid air. As the elements returned to normal, Clarisa's body was slowly lowered to the ground. By the time she had reached the ground, her face looked as it did before. Her clear skin and bright eyes were unveiled. Beverley had called the pastor earlier. When he arrived he waited by the gate for the spirits to leave. Clarisa was blessed and washed in holy water before her body was cold. Hope kissed her mother goodbye…

Following this incident Frank left Jamaica, while Beverley and Cyril continued to write and send little gifts for Hope. In return, Hope would send notes with pictures of her new family. They were like grandparents to her. They even came to Ian's funeral and stayed for three weeks just to be with Hope.

Turn arrived at Hope's graduation. While he was sitting in the audience he noticed Elsa with the kids. He swallowed as, from a distance, he looked upon his beautiful family. After the award ceremony, the sound of flutes filled the air and champagne was handed out. He stood for a while watching Elsa, she looked exactly the same. She couldn't stop smiling, she was telling everyone her daughter had graduated with a full scholarship and honours. She had loved Hope from the minute she walked through the door, when they got back from Jamaica. The children turned and glanced around the room looking for Hope. He smiled as they caught his eye, but they didn't recognise him.

The word was that the prom was due to start in an hour in the school hall. The school had gone all out this year: DJ, decorations, full buffet. The kids had a great time.

After the prom, Hope walked out with the one guy she had dedicated most of her evening to. They got in a boy racer car: you know the type, big rims, full body kit, flames painted on the bonnet. He drove her home and parked up just before he reached outside the house, avoiding the street light. The boy started to put his arms around her shoulders as they sat in the car. She was slightly hesitant but didn't object. A few minutes went by and the boy put his hand on her leg. She tried to move it but the boy pulled her body towards him and started kissing her forcefully. His hands were moving all over her, in and out of her dress. Hope couldn't move. Turn punched through the glass and pulled the boy through the opening. He let out a scream then pushed the boy up against the car to face him. He spun and bent down a little while pushing his back into the boy's chest, held him and pulled him down, dislocating both arms in one move. Hope had fixed herself up in the car and ran out shouting, "Please, don't kill him!" The boy was rolling around on the floor as she began to kick him below his belt. "Not that he doesn't deserve it," she said, "but it wouldn't be right. You remind me of my dad, he would have done exactly the same thing." Still fixing herself up she went on, "When I was little someone tried the same thing, and he came and broke the man's arm." When she looked up Turn was gone. She didn't want to leave the boy on her doorstep so she drove him to the emergency room and took a taxi home.

When Turn got home he told the guys everything, especially how his first born, his little girl, had turned into a nice young lady.

Turn was enriched and ready to go back to the operations room. The guys laughed when they read the police report about the boy with the dislocated arms. Jobs were still flooding in and Hacker navigated the guys to the front door every time. They were able to knock out three, sometimes four jobs a night, with the help of Hacker. Rich and powerful. Unstoppable. But they never lost themselves, they knew what they did was not legal, they were committing murder in the first degree, they had a set-up that not even government projects could fund; they had chosen their lives and one day it just might catch up with them.

Things were on point, running better than planned. Turn decided to focus on the guys that were selling the drugs in the neighbourhood. When they looked into it they didn't realise so many people were out there selling drugs. At first they targeted the guys who sold to the people dealing on the street, hoping to stop the flow of drugs to the users who should know better. They would find and break into their homes and destroy their stash, killing them instantly without hesitation and leaving them to burn. It turned into gangland wars, the only difference being that the ghetto brothers were destroying the stash instead of using it and any money found was taken to the closest charity, home or hospice that dealt with rehabilitation and street clean ups. The dealers started to kill each other not knowing who was doing what. The crew went even further and started destroying the laboratories that were producing the drugs. This hit the drug world hard and major exporting countries refused business. They had torn down the drug world. The guys were away for two weeks with only Hacker as their contact.

When they got back Hacker updated them on what had been happening. He had put it into a report-style pack; attached were letters linked to the same case. There was a serial rapist on the loose. He had been in police custody but somehow escaped and he was now nowhere to be found. They picked up the cars and switched on the trackers which had been designed by Hacker. Morning had just broken as they drove down the hill. Turn had a serious expression. "What if it was one of my own? This man haffi dead." Hacker led them straight to him. He explained that he could see two bodies in the barn, through the heat sensor, but he did not know which one was him. Turn and Flame walked to either side of the barn as Shadow headed to the front. Flame and Turn entered from the side. He had a schoolgirl with him. She was on top of a haystack with her clothes having been ripped away. She lay with her legs apart hanging over the stack; she'd been tied down and was shaking so much it looked as though she was having a fit. The man knew he wouldn't be able to get away with this one. He was wearing just his vest and started to run. Flame spun the rope like a cowboy and caught his neck, the lasso almost choking him as he dropped to the floor with a thud. Flame pulled him to the middle of the barn then Dead gripped the rope. Turn picked up a rusty old pair of shears from the barn wall. Dead was confused. Turn took the shears and chopped at Dead's manhood; the shears were so blunt, he had to snap and snap and snap a few times before it fell off, but it worked in the end. First they put it in his mouth. "Now it's your turn," said Turn, "have ya dinner." They stuffed it down his throat, blocking his airways. Then they cut him up and placed Dead into a small barrel. They left the barrel beside the rubbish bags at the police station. It had a tag on it, which read *This is your rapist, it was an honour to take him out.* News reports made it out to be one of the biggest vigilante killings for over 20 years. Who could do something like this? People were calling radio stations saying all types of things: some people thought these guys were doing society a favour; others thought they were no better than their victims. Some people wanted them dead and some people called them healers for the victims. Others called them freaks and murderers.

The crew looked upon themselves as saviours but in truth they too had wrested with the same question a thousand times. They had come to the conclusion that sometimes bad things must happen for good to prevail. There were not many people in the family, the crew, but each one understood and believed in Turn and his mission. What he said was the law.

Deep down Turn was still concerned about the fact he couldn't read but Hacker made him look at himself differently. Hacker reminded Turn of himself. His young mind was alive with more than just the normal day-to-day routine, he ran through networks like a virus, he was so talented. There was an instant bond between the two of them and they had a lot in common.

For years the ghetto brothers had created a chain of killing. Exterminating the bad guys made them the most wanted and the most hunted. No one knew who they were, even when they were out shopping. It was great. They lived by one code and that was never to say anything to anyone. They had each other to talk to.

6

Things were running smoothly, maybe a little too smoothly. Turn felt that they had done all they could. It was time to move on, take things to the next level. With this in mind he made a suggestion over breakfast and no one really minded. It made sense.

The house was cleared of all computer systems, satellites, keypads and verifiers. They turned the mansion into a hospice; there was plenty of room for at least fifty patients and nursing staff. They fixed the road and cleaned up the cemetery then donated it to the Social Services as a gift. They said it was from an old man who died alone in the house. He had no family to speak of and he didn't want to leave it empty. Social Services weren't in a position to say no, this was just the sort of handout they needed. They questioned nothing and said thank you. The deeds were handed over.

The crew drove all night before stopping in a lively town called Deel. Instead of buying a house as before, they decided to rent. Luckily, a lady had just refurbished a three-floored house and made it into six spacious one-bedroomed flats including the basement. She had put a note in the window of the ground floor flat with her number. Each of the crew called her separately and she was overjoyed to be renting them so fast. All she wanted was some ID, a month's deposit and six weeks' rent in advance. None of that was a problem, each of the guys had several passports and matching driving licences under false names and money was always at hand.

They each checked out the new town and came up with the same conclusion, namely, that they needed to lower the town's crime rate. Hacker had his scanner on constantly and wore it like a Walkman. He heard over a hundred calls an hour, all from people sounding distressed or under attack – rapist, addicts, gangs.

Shadow would spot dealers in alleys and had no fear of the police. Flame would see them wrapped up in their cars, keeping warm as they ate pizza slices and drank coffee, with the person on the radio telling them what was on TV.

Turn was already at home setting up the equipment in the basement flat, which was designated to Hacker. He had run the cables to the roof and set up the aerials and satellites as discreetly as possible. The location was perfect. They were bang in the middle of town hidden by all the hustle and bustle. No one took the time to notice anyone but themselves. The crew would need to be a lot more cautious as they could be found at any point.

The PO box address was re-routed to another and

discreet messages let out to the abused people of the town. Once again the mailbox was soon full. It wasn't long before the guys were doing what they did best. Hacker certainly became an asset and helped in making the crew invincible. Not only were there letters of desperation, there were letters of thanks and appreciation. Maybe being an assassin wasn't all that terrible after all.

The first case in Deel was unusual and the crew hadn't dealt with anything like it before. They had heard about things like this, but being requested to handle the case was a first. It was from a man whose letter was full of hateful and aggressive words. He spoke of his brother-in-law, describing him as a manipulator, an alcoholic, a drug addict, a womaniser and a wife beater. He wrote about the night his sister was beaten badly. The man had left her lying there unconscious for two days, with her children crying at her side begging her to wake up but they were too young to help. Meanwhile he was wasting his money on being entertained in the red light district. Police tried to intervene but his sister feared the man so much she dropped all the charges. After months of unbearable treatment she finally took the three children and ran away, leaving a note to say she was leaving him and didn't want him in her life or the children's lives until they were grown up. He looked high and low for her, sending threats to her mother's house and throwing bricks through her brother's windows. Eventually he found the children in a pre-school on the far side of town. It was during school break. As they were huddling in the school garden, he jumped over the fence and grabbed them. Unfortunately, the children were not missed until break was over and teaching had begun. The school contacted his sister and the police and explained the situation in detail. There was only one witness and he wouldn't speak up as he too knew how violent and manipulative the woman's husband was and feared for his own life. His sister was beside herself with worry and knew instinctively who had taken them. A few days later the children were found; they lay one on top of the other, lifeless. The autopsy showed an overdose of heroine, leading to immediate death. When the report was released on the news, this is when the witness stepped in but it was too late for the children. His sister was so enraged she took her father's shotgun and went to his house but he had already called the police and she was arrested as she shot off the lock of the front door. The police took pity upon her. They knew about the abuse and mistreatment from her estranged husband and now the sudden loss of her children. It had all become too much for her. She was staying with him now, heavily dosed up on medication from the doctor and remaining in her room day and night. It was clear that the man had ruined his own life and lost his wife, so in exchange he had taken the lives of his children to gain revenge on her. Now she had lost *her* life. The only thing that had kept her going was her children and they had been taken from her by the very same man that had destroyed her soul and crushed her world.

The letter spoke a thousand words. There was no need to research this case. It was already high profile; the media were all over it. The man had a highly competent lawyer at his side, well known for his mafia connections, under-the-table dealings and now he was up for a judgeship. Hacker gave a full update to the guys but they didn't wait to hear the end of the report. They all wanted this man and his lawyer dead.

The two men were always in the public eye; reporters, personal assistants, friends, mob members, he was never alone. It was lunchtime. Dead and his lawyer were both in a high class restaurant, owned, run and protected by the mob. It was Flame who entered the restaurant first. He walked through in his chrises suit. To him he looked like a king, tailored from locks to socks, sleek 'n' chic, he moved with ease, almost like Mr Brown on stage. He glided past Dead as he sat at his table, salivating over a nicoie salad, and went on through to the men's room. He glanced over at Shadow standing in his waiter uniform, and flicked his collar. Shadow kissed his teeth, wondering how the rat-looking bwoy got to wear the suit. Flame entered the men's room, making sure the door was closed gently before locking it behind him. He could hear voices. He tapped his left ear, increasing the volume in the transmitter, which was recording back at the zone. The voice decoder identified the three voices as Dead's lawyer, Schnap, the Chief of

Police, Beck, and the number two of the mob world, Paolo. It was obvious they were talking about the case. Flame stayed by the door and listened; they laughed and joked about how Dead was so devastated when his wife left him he wanted to kill himself. What jury wouldn't love that story? They went on to say that Dead's wife would probably kill herself once he was set free and spoke in detail of how many people they had to pay off for this worthless son of a bitch. Indeed, to ensure they had the majority vote of the jury they gave names, times and dates of people linked to various other cases who could be persuaded time and time again to distract or supply them with all types of law-obstructing evidence. They had spoken freely about their crimes and Hacker had recorded every voice, clearly. Flame decided to make his presence known. He walked into the lounge partition of the men's room. They were relaxed and didn't care about seeing someone in there with them. After all, this was a mafia establishment. Flame raised his hand as if to greet the men. They nodded as he continued to the toilet cubicles.

Meanwhile, Shadow manoeuvred around the restaurant floor while Hacker gave the signal for Turn to enter the restaurant. He was dressed neatly but not as overtly as Flame and the rest of the restaurant users. He was at least 20 steps behind Shadow. Shadow approached the table where Dead was sitting and asked if everything was okay. He looked up into Shadows eyes, a little taken by his size, and replied "magnificent". As

Shadow leaned up Turn sat in the chair opposite Dead. He was so concerned by the sweet taste of his food and the last interruption he didn't realise that anyone had sat with him until he looked up for his drink.

Angrily he asked, "Who are you, if you don't leave I will call the owner, do you know who he is?"

Turn looked straight at him. "How could you do that to your own kid?"

Dead was used to outbursts from the public. He replied, "None of your business." With that he got up, looking utterly disgusted, and approached the door. He left the restaurant and walked to the building across the road.

Flame stepped out of his cubicle, cool as a breeze. Hacker had sent a signal indicating that Turn had left the restaurant and was in position. Flame washed his hands then placed more soap onto his palms, leaving a trail of water. He walked out of the cubicle area and into the lounge partition where the men were still discussing the way the law ought to be. He stepped into their area and invited himself into their space. They looked up, each with a cigar in their hand. "Can I help you?" asked Schnap, the lawyer. Flame didn't answer. He stood in the middle of the room with Schnap behind him. His hands spun around, twice as fast as his body, freeing his palms of the luxury soap which flew across the open air into the eyes of Beck and Paolo. He knew he had to disarm them first as they were always carrying a weapon, it came with the territory. He stopped and spun to face Schnap.

"What I am about to do does not satisfy me. After worldwide public humiliation your death should be long, slow and painful but unfortunately you are not the only devil-ridden manipulate that has arisen on this earth so I do not have the time to enjoy the pleasure of watching what you are about to receive. Instead, the bullet inside my gun will deliver you to your maker who will impose your judgement." Schnap was speechless and helpless. His only help was in the room with him, rolling over the floor and crying over the pain eating away at their eyes, debilitated by the very same soap they'd washed their hands with. With that Flame shot them three times, each bullet sending an agonising stroke of pain as they penetrated through his chest and forehead. Schnap was dead. Flame turned to Beck and Paolo. There were two more shots, one for each victim in the back of the head, ripping a hole through the top of their spinal cords and leaving them almost decapitated. Flame returned the chrome Taurus to its rightful place, under his left arm, and unlocked the bathroom door. He made his way out via the back door which Shadow had already unlatched for their departure.

Flame and Shadow linked up with Turn at the sniper position. Hacker set off the fire alarm in the restaurant, which automatically alerted the firemen of Deel. Before the crew knew it the restaurant was being evacuated by the staff. There in the middle was Dead. Turn was about to let off a shot from his rifle when he noticed some of the staff running out screaming; the bodies had been found. The mob members looked around for anyone that could have done this to their brother Paolo. At that point Dead dropped to the floor, Turn had shot him through the ear.

On the way home, Turn was still mystified as to how someone could ever want to kill their own children. Hacker already had the mob's allies listed and everyone that the dirt bags in the men's room had stated were very helpful. The crew were going to clean up the town. They already knew who were the cause of such a mess. The mob.

With every day that went by, Turn would awake with the urge to kill someone. There was so much to deal with. The mob members and their connections couldn't get it together, they were running scared, and yet they didn't know who they were running from. Even though the police records showed a drop in crime and less harassment from the mob, they still had to investigate, and like the mob they too had no idea who they were searching for.

The crew decided to keep a low profile and they did so for some time, only doing jobs out of town and the borough. On the route back from a two-day job, containing seven hits, they saw two guys robbing an off licence. As they were reversing back to the event, they saw them shoot the clerk behind the till. They jumped out of the vehicle like SWAT; the door was already covered before the two guys noticed they had company. Shadow tended to the clerk while Flame flew down the back aisle.

Turn confronted them head on and without mercy he pulled up his foot and let loose. He disarmed the robber and buckled his wrist bone. The man sank to his knees in pain and his partner in crime fell on top of him. Flame had grabbed him from the back and drop-kicked him in the neck. Turn took off the guy's mask. He was dead. When his partner fell on him a shot was released from the gun he was trying to get to and punctured his lung. They looked about sixteen. Turn felt numb at the thought that two boys with so much to learn could be in that place at that time intent on taking another man's life in cold blood, for the sake of a drink and a smoke. The crew knew they had to do it; 'nipping it in the bud' was Flame's usual term for it. The crew knew why they had chosen this sort of life and there was no other reasoning needed as far as they were concerned.

The last incident had caused Turn's mind to start ticking, he thought of his own children. The last time he saw them was when he went to Hope's graduation. One day, he casually asked Hacker if he had received any reports from Aaron lately and with a smile Hacker replied, "Top draw, governor."

Turn sat with a glass of orange juice and pondered over the reports. Aaron was always detailed and gave great descriptions of all the children, so much so that he could visualise them and imagine the type of people they were. He wrote about Hope being accepted into a gracious forensic scientist school, passing all her police academy exams, and how she was now a hard-working detective, admired and respected by both colleagues and civilians, good and bad.

This was unexpected. It seemed that Hope was fighting the same battle as Turn – they just had different ways of going about it. Fatherly instincts rose inside of Turn, he wanted to help and protect his little girl. In all his life he had never felt love like the love he felt inside him when he saw Hope come into the world. Nothing else had mattered, nothing else compared to this feeling. Turn had decided to keep an eye on Hope. He tracked and followed all her cases and even set the bad guys up on a few occasions enabling her to catch them. Of course, she thought she was doing it all on her own, that was the plan. She became highly rated and after several promotions was soon given the title of Chief of Police. Hope was very good at her job. She never gave up, even when all the clues around her led to dead ends. She was persistent and knew how to work the streets, using the bad guys to her advantage.

One day Hope was going through ongoing cases when she spotted a file she had looked at as a trainee. She remembered being intrigued by the coincidental deaths linked to the case; no two deaths were ever the same, but the viciousness and time taken to perform the killing were significant. It was definitely some kind of vigilante warfare. No one could work it out nor could they identify the people responsible for it. Turn was in her life now, that was for sure, it just wasn't the way he had planned it.

Hope had the case on her desk, it was her baby. She made it a part of her everyday duties but after six months she was still none the wiser as to who the culprits were. She did have one thing: a lead, out of nowhere, courtesy of Turn. The lead stated that they were serial killers but they couldn't determine if it was two or three of them. With this to work on Hope made a speech to the press and her colleagues saying that she was going to dedicate her life and career to find these serial killers. She went on to say that she would stop at nothing to catch them. Turn was proud of his first born and kept a low profile as he knew her words weren't spoken in jest.

While conducting his own research Turn soon found out that Hope was a single parent of two children. She had been happily married to a man of great stature, a high-ranking naval officer, one of the best. But he'd been the innocent victim of a drive-by shoot out and his killers were never found. Turn wanted to send a message to Hope and could see no better way of doing it. Turn looked high and low for the driver and shooter of that fatal night. When he did find them, they were already in jail serving time for another crime they had committed. Turn had his contacts inside and knew that he could get the men killed without setting foot around the prison door. Instead, he chose to leave all the evidence on Hope's desk via courier. Inside the envelope were photos, film footage from CCTV cameras, witness statements and much more including a note that said

This is the justice I have done for your husband. He also put a sign at the bottom and ended it *From Turn*. Hope was speechless. She didn't know who Turn was or why he had sent this information to her, let alone where this evidence had come from after all these years. She sent the envelope and its contents down to the lab to check for prints and its authenticity.

Sky had added on some extras to the network – spyware and telephone intelligence. This gave them even more of an edge over the police. With this knowledge the ghetto Boys went back on the road, doing what they did best. As long as Hacker was with them they had nothing else to worry about, they were untouchable. They listened out for the most wanted guys and did their thing. The police were on a twenty-four hour look-out for them. Occasionally, Hacker would pretend to be an officer and send a message over the radio about the 'potentially dangerous vigilantes' as they were known. Conversations would last through the night with many replies coming back supportive. Lots of guys just thought they were talking to another officer from another area and spoke freely about the situation; some just agreed with replies, occasionally someone replied negatively. Someone else would kiss their teeth, showing disgust in the opinion, and soon officers would join in without stating who they were. Hacker enjoyed the banter and recorded some of the conversations. One day he was in the off licence, the one that was robbed by the two young boys that the crew took out. A policeman was asking the clerk how he was doing. He was still torn about that night but showed no sign of who he thought was to praise for his survival. The policeman agreed and even went as far as to say that there should be a department within the police force to deal with certain situations the same way. Hacker could tell that support was high but how many of them would show their support in a court of law? On one hand all the cops wanted the biggest catch of their lives and on the other they didn't. They knew they couldn't do what the guys were doing even if it needed to be done.

The guys had been in town for nearly a year, their faces were becoming familiar but still no one knew who they were or even that they knew each other. Things were getting very warm and police were always circulating. None of the guys really worked, aside from the duties as a crew member, with most of their day-to-day routine being voluntary or charity work. Against this background they set up a learning facility for young kids in order to get them off the street. Offending kids that had been to and come out of prison would be assigned to the centre so they could learn life skills and a trade that would hopefully stabilise their future in society. The centre became well known for its work and was soon listed as the country's number one rehabilitation centre for re-offending youths. Aaron was the front man as with his continuous trustworthy and reliable service to Turn and his family over many years, he was the most obvious choice. The others worked one-to-one with the kids and didn't enter the politics of government requests, curriculums and funding. Although Aaron was listed as the director of the project, he was fully aware that this was a promotion from a man he had no knowledge of. Yet he was inspired and knew never to cross this man he looked up to. He still wasn't sure who was who. Even though Turn worked alongside the youths and got himself as dirty as them, Aaron knew that Turn was the founder of the project and he had given him the power to run the show. He felt privileged. He knew Shadow's voice and was able to show great affection when they met. Shadow was happy to see his telephone friend and didn't expect him to be given such a warm welcome. They were like long lost friends. Aaron never imposed or stepped over the mark. He had no idea who these men were, where they were from and what they did. He could only guess. Nothing was concrete as nothing had ever been confirmed, but his intuition told him that they were good people and he did as he was advised and respected everything that the project did, not just for him but for the next generation. Although he was kept busy with the running of the project, with the permission of Turn, Shadow told Aaron that he should continue with his inventions and bring them into the project. A lot of his ideas were very innovative – someone might take a liking to them, he figured. Of course, Aaron was over the moon and started to introduce his inventions into the project. Turn, Shadow and Flame were true masters of their profession, which was building. They didn't get to do much any more due to other commitments but they found great relief and satisfaction in teaching carpentry and plastering. The youths enjoyed the practical sessions and showed enthusiasm in everything they did. There were many workshops including fashion design, dressmaking and modelling, as well as certificates and qualifications in all subjects. The project was able to use all the connections available to them to get these kids into jobs or apprenticeships, and in many cases university. Some went on to join the army. Whichever route they decided to take, they had all been taught to respect justice and had developed a firm understanding of right and wrong, not just for themselves but in everything they said and did. The youths would leave the project with recommendations and merits that ordinary schoolchildren lacked. The ghetto boys had started something really big. But still no one knew these men were able to become deadly dark assassins when the need arose.

Then one day there was a surprise visit from the Chief of Police herself. Hope spoke highly about the project as Turn sat behind a two-way mirror analysing his daughter. He couldn't believe how she had grown up. *She's a great lady* he thought. She looked like her mum but had all his features and all the charm, intelligence and wit of Elsa. He was blown away because to him she was like a movie star. Hope had decided to join the convoy that was dropping off some youths for the project. They had re-offended twice before signing up to the project so she, along with another officer and a social worker, were monitoring their progress as well as receiving a report on their attendance and attitude. Hope had no idea this project was owned, run and started by her own flesh and blood – the very same man she was currently tracking down for a series of cold-blooded killings. She couldn't fault the project and its positive work so she put her stamp of approval on it and told the team she would be willing to give any assistance they may need.

Hope tried on many occasions to meet the founder of the project and was determined not to leave without congratulating them personally on their insight and their vast achievements. Reluctantly and with a stomach full of nerves Turn entered the hall as discreetly as possible accompanied by Aaron. Aaron introduced Hope to Turn. She didn't comment upon his name as she had already noted that all staff members had an unusual name. She put out her hand to greet him. Taking hold of her hand made him feel special. She congratulated him on his success and asked him how he could have such drive, energy and enthusiasm for the project. Turn remained a man of few words. Instead he subtly changed the subject by asking her similar questions only directed at her own upbringing. Hope found it very easy to talk to Turn and was not offended by his personal questions. In truth, Hope actually felt good talking to Turn about her past as everything was so regimented for her, especially as she was Chief of Police. When Turn asked her about her father, she looked at him as though she knew who he was; at that point Turn felt uneasy as though he was being watched. Before Hope continued she told Turn that he resembled her little brother in some way. Her mumsy had always said that her brother was the spitting image of him. She told Turn that her dad died in an accident when she was small. Turn watched his daughter as she spoke out about her life, her children and being a widow. He didn't want to lose her again. He wished her all the best and told her that his door was always open. After a while a friendship was formed. To Hope he was a remarkable man who didn't compare to anyone she had ever met. To Turn he was being a father to his first-born daughter.

Turn and Hope were now speaking to each other on a daily basis. She was always telling him about her cases and how they were getting on and would always mention her longest standing case. Even though more killings had been done they were no closer to catching the perpetrators. Nothing ever linked any of the killings. Witnesses saw nothing and knew nothing. All the police knew for sure was that these were vigilante killings. Turn would always wish her well in her tasks, he was so proud of her. Letting her down was not an option. During the day he was a well-respected team member of a flourishing project designed to help the community and its children but at night he had to continue with his own mission; it was his life. Hope called Turn one day and told him about a man they had hunted for months despite having collected as much evidence as possible. According to Hope the man had sexually assaulted seven girls in one night. The case was brought forward and the man was sentenced. Hope's frustration was more than evident, they had given the man a minimum sentence and after serving only a quarter of his time they had let him out. Good behaviour they said. Now he was back on the streets harassing the very same girls he had abused. Turn didn't need any more information. Not only had this man been convicted for his crimes and then set free to harass the very same victims, his actions had affected his daughter's sense of justice. He calmed Hope and told her that it was a part of her job and that maybe she should look into stricter regulations that stopped this type of thing. She left the conversation feeling a little better and decided to look for law books to see if there was anything that could be changed or tightened to help change these situations. The next morning Hope was back on the phone telling Turn that the very same man they'd been talking about last night had been found dead. His throat had been cut as he sat in his car outside the house of one of his victims. His hand was full of pictures of the girls as they undressed in front of their windows. Turn asked Hope if she felt this represented justice. "I was not brought up to lie and so due to my position in society I cannot answer that question." Turn agreed with her.

Doing the project and perfecting it made the guys

feel like they had a real purpose in life. The realism of the project and all the people that passed through it with a variety of problems showed the guys that things are possible when they are dealt with. The ones who slipped through the net needed to be eliminated and the success of the centres proved this. When they arrived in Deel, there was no community spirit, everything was being run by drugs and victimisation. Schools were empty, babies on the street by themselves, council buildings shut down, those that could move away did so and those that were not as fortunate soon fell into a life of redemption and poverty. Now with the project and the missions completed by the Ghetto Boys, the town was thriving; new businesses, schools filled with laughter and promise, homes rebuilt, clean streets, police officers involving themselves with the people of Deel. They had put hope back into the lives of decent people. It was flourishing and with that, the decision was made, the crew were going to move on. Somewhere another town was crying out for them and they were willing to oblige.

Turn had briefly mentioned to Hope that his work in Deel seemed to be coming to an end. She wasn't sure what he meant by this until she turned up at the project to see that it was being managed by someone else and had different staff members, a few of which she recognised as its students. She asked the new director where they had gone to. Embarrassed as he was, he told Hope that they had gone to seek out another town that needed them, they were going to start up a sister project with the same intentions as they'd had for this one. However, he didn't know where it was yet. Turn had told him to keep things in order until they had set up and that was what he was doing. Aaron had left detailed reports of funding and statistics, he called twice a week to make sure all was fine and answer any questions but that was it.

Hope left feeling a little disheartened. She had missed speaking on the phone to Turn. But most of all she was upset with herself for not realising that what was now a close friend had told her that they would be moving away and she was too busy in her own world to realise it. She tried to track them down but knew she couldn't. She had nothing but the memory of what they looked like along with the nicknames of the project. To find Aaron was her only hope.

The guys were on the road all day, waiting for Turn to decide where they were going to set up. Turn let destiny decide; as he listened to the radio he heard a report about a boy in a place called Sarfend who killed his mother because she wouldn't give him any money. 'That's where we're going!' said Turn. As they were entering Sarfend, Aaron read an article from a local newspaper regarding the young boy. It turned out that he hadn't stolen the money from his mother, he'd asked for it so he felt he deserved it. When she said no, he was so enraged that he broke the leg of the dinning room table and repeatedly beat her over the head with it until she passed out. The autopsy showed that while she was lying on the floor helpless he continued to hit her with the table leg. It was reported that when he was finished, he took money from her purse to go and buy drugs. The article went on to say that if there was a project in Sarfend like the one in Deel, this boy may have a chance of reintegration and a life. The guys felt that the boy had gone too far, his future was already decided. There was not much in Sarfend; shops closed early and every building looked unattended with open doors and broken window panes. There were a few places that looked very well maintained, the guys had no illusions about who lived in them. Aaron was positive. "Guys, we can set up anywhere, find the landowner of any one of these derelict buildings and tell them we want to buy the property. While it's in this state we can get it for nearly nothing and set up the project. Aaron rambled on and on, the guys loved his enthusiasm, but they were encouraged by other feelings as well as the project.

It didn't take long. Aaron did what he said he was going to do and the owner said they could have it. He had heard of the good work at the project in Deel and welcomed the opportunity to give something to such a worthwhile cause. The elderly man had run far from Sarfend when his daughter was killed by a stray bullet and then his wife died due to a hit and run. He felt he could stay there no longer when his brother was placed into a mental institute and overdosed on his medication. He said Sarfend had destroyed him and his family and he would never return. The drugs had taken over the town, young kids were getting hooked and selling the drugs to their younger friends just so they could pay for their own hit and many people had committed suicide, unable to deal with the way life was turning out for them.

The property was worn down and needed a lot of work, but they used this as a practical task for children and adults of the community who were being enticed to enrol. Many of them didn't have a better choice; it was that or prison. When the youths saw Turn and Shadow they knew there was no room for disrespect and kept themselves quiet and open to all tasks set to them, no grumble, no back chat.

By day the project was doing very well. All the workshops were full and the guys made good use of the very top floor as their home. In the evening everyone would walk about the town promoting the scheme and seeing what the youths were doing on the streets. While Aaron and Hacker walked the streets, Turn, Shadow and Flame were on the lookout for the next victim, eradicating street sellers and petty thieves.

The guys had met lots of people from the community, all of them very helpful and learning to be resourceful. One man in particular was extremely helpful. He told the guys that when he and his wife got divorced she took the children with her leaving him with no access to his own children. He showed great emotion, shedding tears and looking for comfort, so he moved to Sarfend to start all over again. He had no contact numbers or forwarding address and said he would try but his efforts always failed. This made him more depressed. He praised the project and the work it did for the community. He felt it comforting that he could help out in anyway, particularly as he believed that drugs was probably the cause of the divorce. The guys didn't ask any questions. Hacker wasn't so sure; he felt uneasy. Something wasn't right, even some of the kids were unsure of him. A few even flinched when he came too close to them. Hacker didn't like seeing that. He rummaged through the newspapers, files, central database, police records but he could find nothing on him; no name, no pictures, no family, nothing matched. Somehow, Hacker just knew he wasn't telling the truth. There wasn't even a record of the divorce let alone the marriage.

Turn was watching Hacker, he admired this little man. Just like Hacker he wasn't sure about this anonymous man but he kept it to himself. It would be easier to deal with him in one go if something unjust were to happen rather than setting up the crew for a take down. One night he watched how Mr Anonymous persuaded one of the more challenging children to walk him to his car, which happened to be parked quite a distance from the project. When the boy came back to the project he was distraught. He tried to cover up his feelings with anger and indirect abuse, not wanting anybody to see him, thinking it would be better to get into trouble and blame it on his current attitude than anybody guessing that the same man he had helped to his car had rubbed his manhood all over his backside as he pushed him up against the car. After a few hours or so he went to the quiet room and lay there looking at the ceiling until he fell asleep. When he woke it was nearly sunrise, he was curled into a ball crying and shivering in a pool of urine. Turn had stayed close by in the next room but didn't want to invade the boy's personal space, so he kept his distance.

Aaron woke up to the sounds of Flame and Shadow looking through Hacker's things. He hadn't come back that night and his bed hadn't been slept in. They were looking for a clue to where he could be. As tough as they were, Flame and Shadow cared and worried for each of the guys as though their lives depended on it. Bubble gum wrappers, tissues, mates, loose change, nothing they found could tell them where Hacker was. They decided to wait patiently, at least until midday. They washed up and went into the kitchen, the chef was already in full mode. He was sorting out the work stations for the cookery classes, and breakfast was being shared out to plates awaiting the guys. Turn came in and the guys swung round hoping to see Hacker.

"What's up?" said Turn.

"Hacker didn't sleep in his bed last night," said Aaron. Turn assured them he was fine and would be here shortly after opening time. Although he wasn't aware of Hacker's disappearance, Turn was sure Hacker had gone to the man's house to try and find some more information. Sure enough at 8.00am the sliding doors were opened. In first was Mr Anonymous, walking with a spring in his step, he was always the first one inside. A few minutes later the door slid open again; it was Hacker. He walked straight towards the kitchen, cold and starving, soon to be eased by his brothers. He sat quietly and he ate slowly. He was going to have to tell Turn what he saw last night but didn't know how. The table was being cleared, Shadow and Flame had finished a long time ago. Aaron had tried countless times to talk to Hacker but it was clear he wasn't ready. Turn watched the chef, a talented individual, as he put the finishing touches on the cake.

It was nearly half-past nine. Class was due to start at ten so there were a few students already waiting outside. The chef asked them to come into the kitchen to scrub up and down while they waited for the others. They showed their approval of the cake on the table by the use of small gestures such as 'hmmm' and 'yummy'. The chef smiled and took a bow. "Let's see what yours looks like."

Hacker, who was sitting next to Turn, hung over his plate and played with the egg yoke in the ketchup. Turn stood up, looked at Hacker and gave him a playful rap on the cheek before leaving the table. Then Hacker looked at him as he walked towards the door. He finally decided to say what was bothering him. "Turn, I need to talk to you."

Without looking back he replied, "Come on, son, let's

go." Before the door could swing back to its closed position Hacker put down his fork and ran out of the kitchen behind Turn. He could hear the chef shouting after him for leaving his plate on the table and even worse, for playing around with his food.

When they were outside, Turn asked one of the nurses to be discreet as she checked on the young boy in the quiet room. Turn sensed Hacker's hesitation and made it easy on him by letting him know that he knew where he'd been last night, which in turn told Hacker that Turn knew more than he was letting on. *Did he know I was going to do this? Did he know the truth about this man? Does he know what type of man is using our project?* Hacker had more questions than answers but felt comfortable knowing that Turn knew something was up, he wasn't alone!

Hacker told Turn about his suspicions and apologised for not telling anyone about what he was doing but felt that he needed to do it alone. Hacker had spent all of his life in different homes, he'd had to fight and get angry just so that nobody would touch him. It wasn't all sexual abuse, it was emotional and physical: one night he may get beaten so badly he couldn't move the next day; the next he would be blackmailed into saying nothing; the following night he would be sexually abused just to confirm that he needed to keep his mouth shut. For most of Hacker's childhood he'd been subjected to mass degradation by his carers and other housemates. He grew stronger and somehow realised he could make it stop by not giving into blackmail. No matter how much pain he had to endure, his persistence grew as strong as theirs.

Watching the man at the project made him see everything he had tried to leave behind. Here was someone, thought Hacker, who was devious and showed wilful misunderstanding, enough to make people feel like he was very humble and harmless. Everything Hacker had learnt was down to his own experiences. He didn't mind cuts and bruises, they temporarily took him away from his life. As for the electric shocks, they gave him a buzz. He was well on his way to becoming an electronic genius, it was his circumstances that had let him down and the way he allowed it to take control of him. He was young and had no one too look up to or anyone to teach him how to overcome the negative things of life.

Hacker and Turn walked for at least a mile, deep in conversation. Turn watched Hacker go through his range of emotions, almost vomiting when he spoke about watching the man reach his peak from the images on the TV then squirting onto the coffee table covered with pictures of naked children laughing with their mouths open. Hacker felt disgusted with himself for not being able to do anything, amazed by the lack of privacy. He stood still and watched every move from the gap in the curtains. With tears in his eyes he went on to tell Turn how the man took a picture out of his bag. It was a snap of a little boy, no more than five years old and from the area. Hacker recognised the cap that they wore with the uniform and the boy was innocently laughing with his mouth wide open. The man took the photo and rubbed his wilted manhood over the picture until he was erect. Then he gripped the photo, pushing backwards and forwards until eventually he ripped through the mouth. This made him even more excited and he laughed out loud before coming all over the coffee table again, making sure to drain every drop out onto the pictures. Hacker couldn't speak anymore, it seemed so unreal. He felt like the child in that photo and he was that child waiting upstairs tormented by the very thought of being called downstairs next. Turn had always known Hacker's life was a troubled one, it was how they met that told him that, but he'd never seen him like this. He was concerned as he watched him kick over the rubbish bins and smack the post box. He thought of the next mission, maybe it would be more beneficial to Hacker to have him inside with them rather than outside on the radio. It would hopefully act as a sort of self healing. After all, there was no doubt about it: this man was now 'Dead'.

Turn let Hacker tell Shadow and Flame what he thought about Dead. As the days went by the others started to appreciate what it was that Hacker had seen from the beginning. Dead was a slimeball. He watched closely the kids who attended with their parents. Although it was sick to even contemplate maybe he was trying to see if the child was already used to the kind of attention he wanted and was willing to give to them.

Flame's agitation was becoming more and more obvious. He grunted and showed nothing but contempt for Dead. He and Shadow tried their best to avoid him but sometimes it couldn't be helped. Although Dead sensed the hostility around him he was more concerned with the sweet thought of pleasuring himself sooner rather than later. The guys were constantly asking when they were going to be able to put an end to this man's pathological ways but Turn kept telling them to cool, the time would soon come. For his own part, Turn was watching Hacker. He wanted Hacker to be ready for this but he wasn't yet showing any signs that was the case. He was still sending warning signals to the other kids, hoping they would not fall into Dead's trap, and Turn surmised that Hacker thought that a warning would ensure their safety.

A few weeks went by and Hacker was on his usual walk around the centre. He spotted the young boy that had followed Dead to his car one evening. Hacker hadn't seen him for a long time and when he looked at him he was reminded of what he used to look like at that age. The boy, who attended the centre every day, had no real friends. He used to come along with a lady from his school but no one had seen her there for a long time. Hacker felt it his duty to talk to and have a relationship with him even though he didn't know his name. The boy looked over at Hacker as they were walking in the same direction. Although they'd never spoken he really liked Hacker, he admired him, he secretly wished that he could be his brother; it was his main reason for coming to the centre.

The two of them reached the kitchen door and smiled at each other. Hacker suggested ice cream. The boy gave a big smile and closed his eyes. The chef had left the kitchen immaculate as usual. Hacker reached for the bowls and spoons while the boy opened the fridge to choose the ice cream. His mouth watered at the sight of strawberry cheesecake. "That's my boy!" shouted Hacker. They halved the tub and nestled themselves in front of their bowls. As they ate they tried to savour the moment but consciously made sure they didn't savour it for too long as they didn't want the ice cream to melt.

They were just like old friends and had a similar story to tell. It became clear just how much they had in common when they delved into their childhoods and revived dramas of love, hate, betrayal and success. The boy talked of the dark nights when he would lay awake shaking beneath his bed hoping not to be the chosen one. Hacker added that when it was his turn, he would pretend to be asleep and when they touched him he would hit out with real punches as though he was sleep fighting. They laughed with their hands on their bellies.

The ice cream was coming to an end and so was the conversation. It was as though everything was okay when the ice cream was in the bowl. The world was a better place, they let their sorrows walk away with that one bowl of ice cream and now they were scraping the bottom of the bowl. There was no more laughter, nothing left to talk about. They had shared some good and bad things and now the time had come to say goodbye. The pair of them sat for a while longer wondering what would come next. A few minutes went by even though it felt like an eternity until finally Hacker stood and said, "I suppose we'd better clean up this mess." The boy nodded as he picked up the empty tub. They washed and cleared everything away, dried their hands and walked back towards the kitchen door.

Hacker touched the boy on the top of his back as if to give him a gentle pat. The boy ducked so quickly Hacker almost lost track of his hand. But almost immediately everything flooded back to Hacker. It was far too late, he couldn't help him. He was completely damaged by his history and it would hinder him forever. "Don't worry," said Hacker, "you're safe here." But even though the boy knew this he didn't know how to trust anyone. He looked up and briskly left the kitchen without a second glance. Hacker stood in the doorway and watched him leave the centre. He knew what that boy was going through and yet he couldn't change it. He would have to realise that not everyone is bad, some people can help.

Hacker closed the kitchen door and headed for the office. As he reached the top of the staircase he could see Dead rapidly walking out of the centre doors. He knew what the man was up to. "Not this time, it's over!" he shouted.

Shadow ran out of the office. "What's up, who are you talking to?"

By this time all the others were on the landing. Turn walked over to Hacker. "Are you ready?"

Hacker looked up at him and replied, "Yes."

Turn looked at his crew and said, "Get ready, it's on."

Shadow and Flame raised their hands as if to praise the blessed one before squatting and doing a jig, systematically. It was something resembling a rain dance although despite it heralding the start of something serious it was extremely amusing. Aaron had no idea what was going on, his face was full of creases and this made the guys laugh out even louder. "It's on, it's on, it's on!" Aaron wanted to be involved as he was really concerned about Hacker. Hacker was his little brother, no one could tell him any different. What was he ready for and why were those fools doing that dance? Why was he the only one who didn't know anything? He tried to pull Hacker to one side and ask him what was going on but he was swinging himself about the place just like the others. *What the hell?* he thought and danced too. The mood was too infectious not to join in. They'd tell him one day what it was all about, he was sure of it. What was more, the trust he had for these men could not be tampered with. He laughed and started to twist up his body until he was dizzy, taking a few moments to realise he was the last one dancing and the others were disappearing through different doors. He stood in the middle of the room, dizzy, but content.

The Sarfend project was full to the brim, not just with youths but with older men and women, drug addicts and schoolteachers. These people needed some kind of advice or path to follow, to enrich themselves and those around them. Unlike the others, this particular project, for the first few months at least, was used primarily for the rehabilitation of all drug misuse from alcohol to Class A drugs. Counsellors were employed as well as psychologists and nurses. Beds were set up on the far side of the building allowing rough sleepers and those who decided to sweat the illegal substances out of their body to have a secure place to rest.

Although the project was always accessible be it day or night, with full security of course, it was hardly ever completely inactive. Running a mission from the project sometimes felt like their cover could be blown at any minute but those thoughts just added to the excitement. The guys chose the daytime to work out their plans and routes, putting any equipment in the truck. Obviously, no one suspected what was going on, not even 'Dead'. In fact, whatever was going on in his mind kept him very preoccupied. He wasn't the first one in anymore and he left at 6.30 every evening – pronto. Everybody who used the project always had something to do, there was always a reason for their visit so no one took the time to notice anything out of the ordinary. Aaron, on the other hand, watched diligently as always but didn't spot the silver hard cases going in the back of the blacked-out truck. Shadow would watch Hacker struggle to the car with them in amusement. He knew something big was going on but he didn't have a clue what it was.

The guys were on point, relaxed and ready. Hacker stayed close to Shadow, he was eagerly anticipating the hunt. He was sure about it and he knew that no matter what happened in there the guys would look after him come what may. He just didn't know what to expect.

The day had arrived and Hacker was feeling really nervous. Turn had talked him through the plan a thousand times and they had been on observation together for what felt like hundreds of times. During observation Turn would show him where they would enter the house and where they would leave. As long as everything went to plan, he showed him what to do if he wanted to walk away from it. Turn was very thorough; he made sure Hacker was under no illusion about what would happen. In fact the only thing that was decided on the night, at that most crucifying moment, was how they would kill him. Would it be a quick slit to the throat, a slow deliberate cut to his main artery, or would they chop off his overworked parts and make him eat it after watching it roast in an oven or pan. It all depended on how they felt that night and what type of remorse the victim was willing to show. Hacker would go to sleep thinking of the things he would like to do – watching horror movies, for instance. Even though he would cringe at the sight of some of them he would wonder if he could perform such ghastly things on a living human being. The sun was setting and all was well. The guys were chilling out at the back in the conservatory. Flame lay on the decking with his head edged up on the door, looking up at the stars while Turn was chipping the bark of a stick with his carving knife.

The sun had finally disappeared leaving a beautiful multi-coloured sky. Shadow said, 'It's going to be hot tomorrow.' With that Turn stood up with his knife in one hand and his carving of a miniature arrow in the other. The guys made their way to the truck and car using various routes, trying not to draw attention to themselves. Dead didn't live far away so they drove in different directions, parking the car around the corner and placing the truck in a place that could be seen from the house. Hacker jumped out and attached the surveillance cameras to the windows, back and front. He also dropped a little black ball through the post box. With the help of a small remote, this ball enabled them to see inside the house and hear what was being said.

Hacker jumped back into the van. Although it was just the beginning of the night, he was feeling good. The cameras were a little off but they could see the front room and kitchen from corner to corner. The clock showed it was a little after 7pm. It wasn't completely dark outside yet and lots of houses on the road were still alive with lights, music and voices. The guys watched the monitors in the truck. As soon as the picture came up, they saw Dead in front of the TV in his bathrobe. His hair was wet and he was rubbing it dry with a towel. He shifted his gaze away from the TV and turned his head towards the kitchen. He called out, "Come here, boy." A young boy came into view. He was chained up like a convict from his neck to his hands, to his waist, to his ankles, and the chains looked heavy. Dead walked slowly into the front room wearing some kind of rubber-like costume. There was a face mask that was zipped up at the back. The two eye pieces were slit open and the mouth had a zip on it. The choker around his neck held the first point of the chain. The rubber waistcoat was tight with a zip at the back, barely covering his belly button. The pants were just as tight, with a purposeful slit from back to front, exposing his genitals and bottom. The boy walked slowly towards him.

As he reached the front room door, Dead greeted him by saying, "Ah, here's my boy, come and dry my hair." The guys watched as this poor soul walked towards Dead, reluctantly, but with no choice. He took the towel and Dead pulled him towards him, unzipped his mouth and kissed him hard. He zipped his mouth back up and let him go. The boy then started to rub Dead's hair until it was dry. Dead was enjoying it, he was humming to himself. When the boy had finished he stood still and waited for his next instruction. Dead continued to watch the television and when the programme had finished he asked the boy what he had made for dinner that day.

"Fish, chips, steak and kidney pie and pasta bake," said Dead, "mmm." Obviously the man knew that the boy couldn't answer while his mouthpiece was zipped. He pulled the boy down onto his lap, held him tightly then caressed his shoulders and back, asking him why he was not talking to him. He even asked the boy if he was upset with him. He kissed his face all over before unzipping his mouthpiece and inserting his tongue. There was no movement from the boy, he just took what was given to him; he had obviously lost the will to resist. His mouthpiece was zipped back up and he was given a tender squeeze on his exposed bottom before being pushed towards the kitchen. Hacker knew all about being a slave to these sick people, he was truly glad he was out of it. He loathed this guy. He wanted to kill this bastard, this motherfucker.

The guys had to tell Hacker to hold his corner. "We'll be in there soon," said Shadow, "let him get comfortable."

A few minutes had passed and Dead was getting restless. He shouted out for the boy and asked where his dinner was. Before he could shout out again, the boy came out of the kitchen with a tray. It had a plate and glass of juice on it. The boy presented Dead with the tray, it was full of vegetables and what looked like some kind of steak. Whatever it was, Dead was delighted with his meal and gave the boy a little pat on his backside. When he had finished eating he let out an almighty burp and rubbed his tummy. The boy was in the kitchen washing up. He was trapped, both emotionally and, of course, physically. Hacker was feeling bad. Turn could feel the distress in his heart.

The boy had nearly finished wiping around the kitchen sink. When Dead went into the kitchen he stood behind the boy, gently leaning on him before placing his hands on his shoulders and stroking his arms. He used slow and gentle movements. It wasn't long before he was putting his face into his neck, using his tongue to lick between the chains and choker. Dead licked the boy's mask all over. As he undid his robe he continued to rub himself up and down the boy's back. He was getting hotter and hotter and had begun panting. Flame got up and said, "I think it's time now, boss." The crew padded up and took what they needed; this included a portable radio which notified them when anybody other than Hacker was coming with them. They left the truck one by one, the street was still lively. Shadow went through to the back of the house with Hacker tucked closely behind him. The two of them stood on either side of the kitchen window, careful not to disturb the bin and pottery. Flame was at the front door looking for a discreet way in. He used a little card to swipe the inner lock, making sure he didn't make any noise. Turn kept guard by the window, it was barely possible to see his outline. He blended into the dark in his black clothing, clocking the activities inside and outside.

Dead was still in the kitchen with the boy and his robe was now open. He was playing with the boy's penis with one hand and wiping the sperm he had already shot out along the boy's anus. The boy knew what was coming, he gripped the kitchen sink. Dead fumbled and fumbled until he felt the entrance on the tip of his penis. Meanwhile, Shadow and Hacker were taking their time as they slid by the window and peeked into the kitchen.

With one swift push, Dead had entered the boy from behind and let out an almighty roar. As he stood up straight he looked out the window, his eyes opening wider with every push. It was at this point he noticed Hacker. The tears were streaming down his mask but between the pain and the feeling of disgust he began to think he was imagining things and that Hacker was just an illusion.

The potted plant came through the window like a 200mph baseball, just missing the side of Dead's face. He dropped to the floor in a panic and asked the boy what was going on. Shadow watched Hacker's unorthodox entrance, a little noisy but it did the job. Hacker was fuming. He had caught a glimpse of what was happening through the window. His eyes had met with the boy's. The tears clearly showed his pain, hurt, humiliation and desperate need for help. The pot was the only thing he could think of to stop the situation from going any further.

When Flame heard the noise, he decided to put his foot on the door to finish off the unsuspected entrance. After observing that no one had been alerted by the noise, Turn entered.

Dead was now under the kitchen table, still shaking. The boy was slumped over the sink, now almost delirious. Shadow and Hacker stepped in through the back door. Next to it was a litter tray and an old blanket, which was full of bloodstains and vomit. They stepped over the blanket and met Turn and Flame at the kitchen door. Shadow turned to Hacker and told him to make sure the house was secure and went on into the front room to prepare some of the tools. Turn picked up the table and put it on the other side to where Dead lay in shock, unable to lift his head. "Take anything you want," he said, "my money is in my wallet but please don't hurt me." Flame reached for the collar of his robe and pulled him into the front room. Hacker had closed the curtains and turned the TV up a little so as to drown out any sounds. Turn followed him, kicking the man's legs when he tried to struggle.

Hacker came downstairs and reported that everything was secure. He was feeling a little more in control, he knew this was the end for Dead. Shadow told him to check the kitchen. He went through and closed up the window blinds. As he turned to lock the back door he saw the boy huddled into a ball on the dirty blanket. He was crying. Hacker didn't want to trouble him. He went into the sitting room and found something in the bag that would free the boy from his chains. He returned and removed the chains, unzipped the mouthpiece and then went to unzip the mask but the boy flinched. This told Hacker he wasn't ready to reveal himself just yet. He stepped back cautiously. He didn't want to make the boy any more nervous so he turned the light off and went into the front room, leaving the door open.

Flame was standing over Dead's head. He was still rolled up and trembling, thinking that they were there to rob him. Turn walked around the room picking up all types of perverted paraphernalia. He threw them over to Shadow, each item followed by a kiss of the teeth. Shadow look at the items in disgust and threw them at Dead's head. It was like cricket practice, making sure not to miss the wicket. Flame laughed at every hit. Hacker was looking at the same people but he had never seen them like this before. He wasn't shocked nor was he offended. He knew what they did was right, the only pain they brought was given to the one who had given it to so many others. He didn't think his admiration for them could be any more than what it was but it was growing. In his eyes they were nothing less than heroes. Hacker started to feel the strength inside of him and in a strange way this was reinforced by seeing the way Dead trembled. Watching him flinch and beg brought back memories but now the shoe was on the other foot and that felt good.

Turn saw Hacker watching Dead receive lick after lick from Shadow's unfailing forearm. He screwed up a picture and tossed it over to him. He didn't see it coming but caught it nevertheless. He opened it slightly and saw a small face then tightened it back up quickly into a ball and hurled it through the air towards Dead's head. Bullseye! He smiled, looking up at Turn for more. Turn saw Hacker's enthusiasm. Although it was his choice to come, he didn't want this to be something that would rule him.

They left Dead on the front room floor, with Flame

taunting him. Flame had one foot on a length of hair so Dead couldn't move his head and a thick piece of rope in his hand. He whipped him ferociously as he writhed around the floor, spitting on him when he tried to shout out. Turn, Shadow and Hacker walked around the rest of the house looking for anything that might show them that Dead had any more children in the house. Upstairs was a child's dream: bright colours, toys, computer games, costumes and posters. It was completely different to the world downstairs. Hacker checked the wardrobes and underneath the beds. Aside from droplets of blood there was nothing there. They checked the store cupboards in the hallway – nothing. The bathroom was a walk-in washroom; no bath, just a shower, sink and toilet. The bedrooms were covered in pictures. In one closet there were more chains and rubber attire with some whips placed in a uniform manner along the inside of the door. A few were covered by a musty smell and the door showed the remnants of blood. With red voile covering the windows and cuffs on the corners of the bed the bedrooms were ready for all types of action, a home boudoir kit.

All the rooms had air fresheners hanging from the ceiling. It was quite strange as they didn't really smell. There was a little hint of a stench but the dangling fir tree fresheners helped to cover it up. Turn felt this to be strange. He looked at the ceilings and examined the corners. Shadow walked around tapping the walls while Hacker looked for the hatch that led to the attic. He shouted to Shadow to give him a bunk up, the hatch was in the bathroom. Shadow stood on a towel so he wouldn't slip on the damp floor and put out his hands for Hacker to step into so he could reach the hatch. Hacker pushed it open. Some kind of sticky substance was holding it down but it wasn't hard to lift the lid. Hacker pushed it to the side. Shadow pushed Hacker up some more and rested his feet upon his shoulders. Hacker's top half was immersed in the darkness of the attic. The smell was unbearable. Turn asked Hacker to tell him if there was anything up there. Hacker, half choking from the smell, shouted back that it was too dark to see anything but he didn't feel good about it.

Turn walked back to the children's room, which was at the top of the landing. He stood in the middle of the room. Although it was full of bright things, there were strong vibes of pain and sorrow. He crossed his arms and held himself until he heard Shadow call out. He went back to the bathroom – pronto. It was immediately clear what had alarmed Shadow. There was a steady flow of blood coming from the attic opening. "Hacker!" "Hacker!" shouted Turn. "Shadow, get him out of there!" Shadow held onto his legs and dropped him down onto his shoulders. Hacker felt like he was in some kind of bad dream. He was coated in blood and had a foot in his hand. Turn pulled Hacker down from Shadow's shoulders, placing him on the floor, propping him up against the wall. Shadow put out his hands, Turn was going up next. He had to see what was happening up there.

Flame was in his element as he tortured and taunted Dead. He didn't notice the boy watching him through the hinges in the doorframe. Dead was almost unconscious from exhaustion. A couple of times Flame was sure he could see Dead getting aroused from the whipping so when it was lit he stumped out the fire, so to speak.

Turn looked down at Hacker rolling off the wall to the floor before putting his head into the attic. He knew from the smell what he was going to find but the light from the torch showed him just how bad it was. He saw the faces of babies and young children. He saw hands and feet, arms and legs discarded along the floor. In some spots there were small heaps. Flesh and odd bones were randomly spread about the place. Turn was astonished at the sight of it. He knew what Hacker was feeling was well out of his bounds of sanity. He would have to take special measures to make sure this didn't harm his wellbeing. Maybe it wasn't such a good idea to have him come along on the ride.

Shadow let Turn down. "Boss, what's up there?" Shadow watched the despair turn to rage on Turn's face. He strutted to the door, bent down and leaned Hacker back up on the wall, as by this time he was lying in his vomit. Turn stood and looked over him for a brief moment before storming back into the hallway to go downstairs and straight to Dead. Shadow found a clean towel and some smelling salts in the bathroom cupboard. Then he soaked the towel in some water. He brought Hacker around with the salts and cleaned him up with the towel. Hacker looked up at him, his eyes red, his mind swimming with thoughts. *This just can't be real.* Shadow wasn't going to change that for him. Protecting Hacker was the overwhelming priority of this mission, for Shadow there was nothing else more important.

Turn's head was spinning. All he wanted to do was kill Dead, chop him up and walk away but he didn't deserve such a short sweet killing, he wanted it to be really painful. Something that Dead would remember when he arrived at the gates for his judgement. Turn wanted him to remember what he had gone through and still feel the pain in every part of him, begging for someone to put an end to the suffering. Although what Turn was doing was not really commendable in the eyes of God, he felt differently. He knew these people deserved to feel what their victims were feeling and when his judgement came he would stand by his word and his doings. He wasn't fighting his inner demons anymore. Turn was living the life he knew he was born to live.

Turn was balancing on Dead's kneecaps. Dead, afraid to move, stopped wriggling. He opened his eyes slowly as he looked up. Because his sight was blurred it took a while for Dead to realise who was standing on him.

Shadow made his way downstairs with Hacker. The salt and water had sorted him out. Although he wasn't sure if what he saw was real, he stood and gave Shadow a look of embarrassment and then thanks. Shadow asked Hacker to sit on the bottom step and told him to stay there until he was ready or it was over. Hacker sat and nodded.

Dead looked at Turn with his eyes wide open. He was stunned but managed a brittle hello. With clumps of hair surrounding his boots, Flame replied, "Hello." Dead turned his eyes to the man with the rope in his hand. He wasn't sure what was happening. He recognised these people and had even thought of them as friends. Why were they doing this? Dead was sure no one knew his secrets, he was sure he was never obvious with his desires, he wondered where the boy was and if he had said anything. But how could he? He was locked in the kitchen chained to the floor day and night unless he was in the house. Dead was befuddled.

Turn didn't move. His deep-rooted intimidating ways made Dead wet himself several times. Flame stepped back. Turn was in a no-holds-barred zone, he sensed something was amiss. The guys must have seen something upstairs they weren't expecting. Shadow's face was a mixture of hate and disgust and when he saw Hacker sitting on the staircase he knew it was bad.

From the back of his belt band, Turn produced a small knife. He held it high, it was pointing at Dead's chest. Turn started to speak. Things that really only made sense to him. Things that came into his mind about why he was here. What he saw upstairs, who he thought all those pieces belonged to and the dirty things he knew took place in the house in which he was unfortunate enough to find himself. He dropped the knife. It was sharp and chipped the skin. As Dead tried to dodge the blade, Turn bent so that he could keep his balance. Dead was back in a lying position. Turn pulled out another knife, a little bigger than the last one. As before, he held the knife in the air and dropped it over Dead's chest. As Dead leaned up and over, the knife caught his shoulder, slicing off the skin along his bone. Now exhausted, the man lay back down only to see another, bigger blade heading for him. He tried to free himself from under Turn's boots but both kneecaps were disjointed and he dropped back in agony. Again the blade dropped into his chest. He held his chest, tears falling, he was pleading for mercy. But Turn was indifferent to Dead's pain and he continued talking while still balancing on Dead's broken knees. There was a moment's silence. This made Dead stop crying and he opened his eyes. Above him was a butcher's knife. Dead squirmed and wriggled about the floor, begging Turn to stop. He pleaded with him, telling him he would change.

Turn stopped talking and looked down at him. He was talking a good game. Forgiveness was big in the eyes of God and Dead respected that. Dead admitted that the bodies in the attic were his family, siblings, cousins, wife, children and friends. He loved them but he longed for someone to talk to about his life and infatuations. He also loved the look on their faces when he told them, that was the best part, but he knew after he had confessed to them that he had to kill them. His children were bringing too much attention home so he put them in the attic too. Turn was slowly bringing down the knife. He didn't like Dead and he wasn't going to let him get away with all that he had done but he was going to hear him out. Dead was the voice of so many sick people out there. If one thing he said could help the guys to identify a predator of his kind without stalking them, saving time and people's lives, Turn was willing to listen for a while.

A few minutes had gone by. Dead remained in the same position, unable to move due to Turn's determination not to step off his kneecaps. Flame couldn't understand why Turn was still listening. He hoped he wasn't being sucked in. As Flame moved in a little closer, Turn raised the blade again. Shadow gasped and Dead watched in horror as the knife was raised above him. He started to get frantic again and shouted out that they could have the boy. Turn's face switched. Dead knew it was the end. As the knife left Turn's fingers there was an almighty roar from the kitchen. It was the boy. He ran towards the knife full of rage then prevented it from piercing Dead and it dropped to the floor. Dead praised his boy and told him to call the police. The guys stood still, unaffected by this sudden interruption. The boy picked up the chopper from the floor, still in his rubber attire. He looked around the room. Dead was still praising him, coaxing him to help him while crying in pain. Hacker was leaning up by the doorframe observing. He didn't want to get involved, he was fine just watching. As much as he wanted to have some kind of input he knew it wasn't in him.

The boy looked around and caught Hacker's gaze, just as he did through the kitchen window. He unzipped the back of his head mask. Dead shouted at him to leave his mask alone and do as he said. He was now wavering, the pain was unbearable. Hacker stood up straight away from the wall. The boy was determined not to lose direct eye contact with Hacker. He gently removed the mask, peeling it from back to front. His ruffled hair gave him away. Then his red cheeks. It was the boy from the centre. Before anything could be said, a tear fell from his eye as he looked at Hacker. Flame moved towards him. He threw down his mask and roared out before lifting the chopper and flying towards Dead's chest. Dead tried to push him off but every time he raised his hand or arm, the boy would slice it, drawing blood from all angles. Dead was limp. He had lost a lot of blood. Turn stood down and let the boy finish off what was left of Dead. He chopped with both hands, grasping the knife tightly. Dead was no longer recognisable and the chopping was slowing down. The boy was covered in blood and shivered at the realisation of what he was doing to the man who had held him in captivity and abused him night and day. He had even witnessed him killing his own daughter. Turn reached out his hand to the boy but he did not take it. Hacker walked slowly into the room to see flesh and brain splattered everywhere.

He bent down next to the boy and waited for him to look at him. Then he reached out his hand to him. The boy took it and they both stood up. Then, a little shakily, they left the room. Hacker put him on the staircase and followed the same steps as Shadow.

The guys wrapped up their tools and equipment. One by one they made their way to the van. Hacker took the boy in the car, wrapped him up in a clean blanket and they drove for a little while in silence. Hacker took him back to the project, where he had a shower and put on some clean clothes. The local hospital was only a few minutes' drive away. After some gentle persuasion he agreed to go but if he was going to have to go then he wanted to go to the next town. Hacker agreed. Turn gave Hacker some money and several numbers of some places where the boy could grow up safely.

It wasn't long before the brutal murder of a local man was plastered all over the news. That was the first time that when they dug a little deeper they realised that it was more than just a local man. There was no evidence to go on and so it was placed in the file with the rest of the vigilante killings.

Two years passed by and Hope was still in search of her serial killers. She continued to plot spots and areas on the map. It was difficult but she persevered, knowing this case would make her career. She left no stone unturned and followed up every lead. Turn was never far behind Hope. He wasn't worried about the leads she was following, he just liked to watch her and try to figure out her thoughts and her next move. She influenced him and he loved it.

7

Things were getting hotter than usual. The police had sent out some strong messages to anyone who might be suspicious of friends or family. They showed the map that Hope had devised of all the areas in which the killings had taken place. They spanned the country and were accompanied with various dates and approximate times. But nothing suggested it was them, there wasn't even a link to show that the killings were only happening in the areas they had settled in. Witnesses couldn't tell who the killers were but Hope knew better. One witness explained that if it were not for the help of these people she would be dead, she even went on to say they were not murderers, they were guardians.

Although the project was in full operation it was literally running itself. The volunteers and family units that attended lived by a policy of each one, teach one, and with the correct foundation and moral standing given by the project it was a blessing to see Hope in all of them. This aside, there was always a second thought:

what if they got caught? All the crew except for Aaron left England for the U.S. Aaron stayed behind to watch over the projects and set up some smaller centres across the country.

They found America to be a totally different world to England. The people were open and not only talked a lot but lived without fear. Although crime was statistically worse, they didn't live cooped up or as victims of their society. Gun shops and army stores dominated the streets. You only needed to show a certificate of US citizenship to buy any gun you could afford and the guys took every opportunity in delighting themselves with body armour, full leather army boots, automatic weapons, rifles and anything else that caught their eye. To them it was like a big toy store. One of the gun shop owners saw the kind of guns the guys were buying and gave them the name of a gun school. It was well known for its links to the Navy Seals and CIA teams across the country. They had trained the best and were specialists in long shots and hunting. One phone call and they were in. The guys chose to live on site for six months and trained themselves in all categories from territorial tactics to SWAT Team protocol. They had grown up with guns in Jamaica but they didn't excite them as much as knives. Turn said it was cleaner but America was a world of guns. They had no choice but to use what their enemies would be using against them – this, along with all the knowledge they already had. The ghetto boys were a force not to be toyed with.

America was huge. Information could be found anywhere, everything was easily accessible to anyone who wanted it, no questions asked. It didn't take long for the guys to find what they were looking for. Lists of crooks, wanted and hunted; what they'd done and how long they'd been wanted; who wanted them, their last location; personal identification and enhanced pictures of the perpetrator showing them in various disguises.

Tall buildings made up the city, which was covered with bright lights and advertisements. Rooftops and scaffolding were the perfect place for the guys to watch their desired targets. Shots were easily taken and victims were taken out as they walked through the busy streets, night or day, shot down like a bird in the sky. Snipers. The best.

The guys would rent motels for a couple of nights at a time. The equipment they used was minimal: rifle with high scope lens, silencer and light adjustable goggles. Specialist needs were never a problem as there was always someone on the street who could tell them where to find it. What they didn't know was that Hope had been asked to go to America for a convention, where she would give a speech to the chiefs of several precincts. She was also invited to do a routine visit to one of the stations, to see how things were run, to look into some cases and follow a detective around for the day.

It was 6.35am and Hope was woken by the sound of the telephone. It was Detective Grant. He was up, ready and on his way to a homicide. He gave Hope the address and said he would meet her there.

Hope pulled up in her rent-a-car. There were flashing lights, not just from police cars but from a pack of reporters. The victim was lying dead in the middle of a road. He had received a bullet to the left side of his head, two inches above his ear. The detective greeted Hope with a large cup of coffee. He explained that this was the twelfth murder in two weeks. The killing was the same, a bullet to the head, two inches above the ear. The only thing the victims had in common was that they were all on America's most wanted list. On returning to the station Hope spoke to the Chief about the spree of killings and her case in England. Nothing really seemed to match. They resembled the vigilante killings and all the victims were wanted but they had witnesses and the killings varied. Knife wounds were the main cause of death but there was suffocation and mutilation. Although the match was not identical Hope felt that her assassins had crossed the water and by a twist of fate she had ended up in the same town. She was sure of it. Hope used her gift of gentle persuasion on the Chief and he allowed Hope to carry on with some investigation work herself while she graced them with her presence. Detective Grant showed Hope the places she needed and took her on all his call outs. Before long the F.B.I. and the C.I.A. were working alongside each other. The hunt was on.

Turn felt something was wrong. Jobs were flowing in

and the kills were easy; there was a lot to do. Fifty-two states weren't going to be easy for them to clean up especially while Turn insisted on lying low.

They had exterminated America's most wanted list and after prioritising their own list from all the jobs they had received, Turn let the crew know he would be shipping their equipment back to the UK via Thailand. "Keep what you need," he told them, "and pack the rest. When the list is successfully completed we will return to the UK." It would be too hard to flee America if things got hot for them. It was the best thing to do.

Hope checked every report and every crime scene. The killings were so clean compared to England. Hope was beginning to think that she was barking up the wrong tree. She packed her bags and left for England.

The flight was due to leave at 12.15pm, searches were full on and security was real tight. Turn handed over his passport to the clerk. He looked across the hall and saw Hope. This made him close his eyes as though he was dreaming but when he opened them she was still there. She looked cool and relaxed, a little distracted, but calm. He wasn't sure how he was going to explain his presence but he was happy to see her. Hope turned around and saw Turn. She ran and gave him a hug. As always, she was elated at the mere sight of him and she asked him what he was doing there. He knew the question was coming. He explained that he was looking into starting a new project there and that he had come over to see some people who were in charge of homeless shelters and single parent community centres. Hope was excited for him. She spoke of her trip from beginning to end and felt so comfortable to be with him. She was able to talk about anything, to get her mind in order, and it made her feel good. She always spoke freely with Turn and was sure he was just being polite when he sat and listened. She told him he was a great person and that she really respected him. She was taken back when he said, "I'm not who you think I am, I'm not as nice as you think." He was smiling as he said it but the comment made her think. At the end of the trip they said their goodbyes and vowed to speak to each other soon.

The guys easily settled back into UK life. Hacker had made sure everything was ready for them. "Let the killing commence!" he said. The guys did their thing, the only difference was that they used their rifles; they felt it would quicken things up as it was so easy. The wanted list was wiped clean and letters were down to a minimum. Hope was not feeling good about this, she had just seen the same thing she saw in America; a bullet to the head two inches above the ear. Now it was impossible not to see the similarities in the killings. MI5 and C.I.A. were not impressed. They joined in the search and listed a silhouette of the most wanted list, with no name and no description. They had no idea who or what they were hunting. It was like the ghost of a shadow. Sometimes the crew didn't know who they were either as they had been killing for so long they now took their way of life for granted. They had created an alter-ego that came out when the heat was on. They were passionate hunters.

Things were better than before. Crime was at an all time low and the centres were flourishing. Within the eighteen months they were in America, Aaron had set up another four centres in various parts of the country. They were always the roughest and darkest places he could find. He managed to keep the government away from the operation by only accepting donations. He had to be seen to be accepting something otherwise, even though the centres showed remarkable results, the government would have deemed them to be money launderers and cults – anything to cause a disturbance. Aaron was sure to pay the taxman everytime he received money from Turn. In fact he even received a tax return for having paid too much. The centres were million pound organisations. Nothing was spared and the people who used the centres were given everything they needed from counselling to medication. All for free. All that was asked of them was that they should spread the word, come if they need to and help out when they could. It was always better, they believed, to see a recovering addict telling the youngsters about their experiences rather than an over-educated counsellor telling them what was right and what was wrong.

Turn was really impressed. He had a vision and Aaron had made it a reality. Flame turned the corner and there it was; the first project, the mother of all centres. Aaron had added on an extension and made it into a reading area. The roof was made of glass, bringing in a flood of light and making the room uplifting. There was a storyteller that read aloud a chosen story at 12 and 5. The centre attracted all types of attention and sometimes those storytellers were well-known musicians or actors.

Turn stepped in with bags of goodies. Flame and Shadow were already inside, making jokes and greeting old faces. No one knew they were coming, it was just a surprise visit. Turn walked around, taking everything in. He stopped outside the office just as the door was opening. Aaron was coming out along with Hope and a few of the volunteers. He was happy, anxious, elated, and cautious. He didn't know what to do. He wanted to jump all over Turn like a dog who hadn't seen his master all day, but eventually it was Hope who stepped forward with a big hug. "Long time," she said, "I haven't seen you since we left the airport, how have you been?"

Turn looked at Hope and said, "I feel good, how about you?"

"Well, after wrenching your ear off on the plane, I got a few things in perspective...we must catch up! I just popped in to see how everything was going. A few of the volunteers wanted to speak to me about a few things that we may be able to change for the whole town. You know, a few more patrols, home visits, that type of stuff. How could I say no after this centre gives so much for little and nothing? If you're going to be in town for a while maybe we can meet? I promise I won't talk your ear off."

"Sure, just let me know when," Turn said. With that they said goodbye and the volunteers showed her out. Aaron stood still with a warm smile on his face, still not sure if he should hug Turn or not. Turn stepped into the office and closed the door. As he turned around, Aaron flew to him like a lost child. He respected Turn like a father. He didn't ask questions and stayed loyal, fighting to fulfil Turn's every dream, no matter what the cost. He began to feel his emotions overcome him. He let go of Turn and kept his head low as he fought back the tears. Turn remained silent. He put out his hand and rested it on Aaron's head. He felt a bond with Aaron as he did with Hacker. He was a son to him, someone he silently depended on, he wouldn't have left the project and its development in his hands if he didn't trust him. With Turn's hand on his head, Aaron felt warmth and strength enter him. He stood and welcomed his boss back home like a man. They spent the rest of the day on the roof watching passers-by.

Money was building up. Even the offshore accounts could be looked upon as suspicious. Something else needed to be done. The guys had always said that staying in the UK was only for the short term – make enough money, live good and be gone. Flame, Shadow, Hacker and Aaron sat at the table while Turn explained his next vision.

Within a week the guys were on a plane to Jamaica. Aaron and Hacker took a little while to adjust to the heat; this amused Flame no end. They explored the island to find that things had changed but not for the better. Flame and Shadow were haunted when they saw families sleeping beneath the same zinc roof *they* used to sleep under. It was these very same people they took with them on their journey.

It was nearly midday when the guys came across some land. It looked as though it wasn't being used and no one was tending to it. They asked the stranger if he knew anything about it or who owned it. The little boy told them it belonged to the government. They tried to sell it but the developer's price was way too low.

"No problem," said Turn. They all went back to the hotel. Shadow ordered a deluxe family suite for the strangers and said he would be going down for dinner at seven. If they wanted to join him they were welcome. Although hesitant, as they did not know kindness, they thanked Shadow for his offer and went to their room.

Turn didn't go to dinner. He left a note saying he'd see everyone bright and early in the morning. He took the jeep and drove around the island he called home, soaking in the fresh air, sweet breeze and the laid-back life. Before he knew it, he was driving on familiar roads. There it was. Cyril and Beverley's home, just as he had left it. The only thing different was the gate, which had been completely changed. He pulled up outside and noted how quiet and peaceful it seemed. Then he thought of the moments he had experienced in the house. One of his happiest moments was coming home with Hope in his arms and Clarisa by his side. He was a dad and he felt proud. He remembered feeling as though he really belonged. He stepped out of the car and opened the gate. He walked over to the outhouse where he and Clarisa first stayed as a family with Hope. It looked the same. There were pictures on the wall of the three of them. It was neat and clean as though it had been prepared for him. He sat for a while on the chair he had made while Clarisa was pregnant and rocked to and fro. After a while he started to doze off and was unaware of Cyril entering the room. Cyril sat on the bed and watched him as he lay back in the chair. He just wanted to look at him. It wasn't long before Beverley could be heard fussing around outside looking for Cyril. She came into the outhouse and saw him sitting on the bed then gently asked him if he was all right. He looked up at her and said, "Our son is home."

She turned slightly and saw Turn in the corner of her eyes. She couldn't help the tears. They were both certain he was dead after the police found the van. Elsa wrote and sent pictures of the children regularly but it only soothed the pain of losing Ian. Cyril and Beverley lay on the bed as still as they could, trying their hardest not to wake him. With joy in their hearts and tears in their eyes they thanked the Lord for bringing their son back home to them.

Early morning had come. Turn opened his eyes slowly, he hadn't slept like that for a long time. He blinked repeatedly until he could see clearly and there he saw the two people who had saved him from himself and all evil. The two people who had taken him in with no questions and given him a chance, making him a part of their family. He got up slowly and crept towards them. They were wrapped in each other's arms, smiling, content. As he got closer he could see they were dead. He dropped on his knees and begged the Lord to keep them safe with him at all times. He went into the house and took out Beverley's favourite white linen voile and put it over them then gently closed the door and left. As he drove away he felt blessed to have shared their last breath with them in the outhouse. When he arrived back at the hotel, before meeting with the guys, he rang for a doctor to attend the house and get back to him as soon as he could.

Everyone met in the lobby. The strangers looked clean and enthusiastic for their drive to the government building. Turn wasn't sure as to what the outcome would be and his mind was elsewhere but he entered the building with the father of the family. He was still unaware of his name so he called him Zinc. When they got inside, the air conditioning was so cold it felt like frost was biting. Zinc nearly fainted with the sudden change of temperature. "Blood clart," said Zinc. That was the first time Turn had heard him speak, he laughed. They approached the desk and asked for the person dealing with the site by Blue River. The lady sent them to the 3rd floor to speak to a surveyor. Jenkins greeted Turn at his office door then offered Turn and Zinc a seat. As he walked around his desk he spoke about the Blue River site. He highly recommended it. He admitted it was pricey but said it was more than worth it. Turn asked how much it was but Jenkins wanted Turn to make him an offer. They drove to Blue River to look over the site, it was bigger than Turn had predicted. It had roughly seven miles of beach front attached to it and by the way Jenkins had described it there were more acres at the back but they couldn't access it as the land was seriously overgrown. Jenkins spoke freely about what he would do if it was his piece of land but this wasn't a money-making venture, this was going to be a haven for him and his crew. Turn let Jenkins speak away, careful not to say a word until the time was right. It didn't take long. Jenkins got so carried away he said how much it was worth. Turn agreed and placed Jenkins' hand in his to seal the deal. Jenkins wasn't sure what happened, but he was happy to be selling the property at the correct price. Turn did a money transfer as soon as he got back to the office, he signed the deed and was on his way. He gave Jenkins a little something to ensure the paperwork was correct and was dealt with properly then returned to the hotel with Zinc.

Turn told the guys what he had done. "But what are you going to do with it?" asked Hacker.

"We are going to build several detached houses, five in fact, with several cottages along each end."

"Five houses?"

"Yes, five, one for me, one for you and one for Shadow, Flame and Aaron. One of the cottages will be given to Zinc."

"Zinc, err, who's that?" Hacker didn't even catch on to the fact that there was a space for a house allocated to him.

Turn looked over to the far table where the strangers were eating. "I didn't know what to call him and Zinc just seemed fitting," Hacker chuckled.

Aaron smiled and thought of a home in Jamaica next door to his best friends. He wouldn't have dreamed of this in a million years. The rest of the day was spent on the site with their backs to the water. They looked up on the site at blueprints and imagined pictures.

Turn spoke to Zinc alone. He knew Zinc was a man full of pride, which was dented because he couldn't feed his family. Turn explained to Zinc what he did in the UK with his projects. He said that he wanted to build the cottages so he could send some of the people who used the centre with their families to stay for a week. He asked him if he would help him set up the cottages and maintain the properties. He would pay him a grand wage and of course he could choose which one of the cottages he wanted as soon as they were finished. Zinc said nothing but the promise of having a home was too good to resist. He had already seen how Turn did his thing when they were with Jenkins and he was impressed. He respected them for taking them from the gutter and putting them into a hotel room. He had fed and clothed him and his family. He stayed silent because of his pride.

Turn didn't want the Blue River site to be full of

tourists, he wanted a family place that wasn't overcrowded and where the children could walk free. All amenities would be available to everyone and it would be fully staffed. There would be a restaurant and small shops with all necessities at hand. Turn was determined to make this work and did not spare any expense. The guys were leaving at the end of the week and everybody had to have the design of the house that they wanted ready to give to Zinc and the foreman. Turn was going to stay on a little longer just to make sure things were in hand. It was also important for him to be a part of building his own home, his empire, his resting place.

Before Turn could get on with Blue River and put his heart and soul into the development he knew he had something important to sort out. He had heard from the doctor that Cyril and Beverley had died of natural causes. They were old and it was time. He made sure that their children were contacted and paid all outstanding bills including the funeral. He paid his last respects at the morgue and was happy to see they were still smiling. When he left he gave the funeral directors a large sum of money. Turn wasn't one for funerals, for him life was about living for the living not the dead but still he wanted to make sure that the funeral was full of beauty and grace no matter what happened or who was there.

Before the guys left for the airport, Blue River was thoroughly cleaned and the foundations were already in place for the main build. The journey back to the UK was quiet even though most of them were thinking about the same thing. Aaron, however, was just sketching. Without Turn returning back to the UK with them, they had no one to ask what they were supposed to do with their new beach homes. Nevertheless, their eerie expressions and smiles kept the hostesses amused and not even the fact that the plane had to circle four times because the rain was too heavy for them to land could dampen their spirits.

8

Blue River was structurally complete and Turn had played a big part in finishing his resting place. When they had finished the roof Turn sat up there for nearly an hour, looking at the water with a big smile on his face. All that was left to do was the interior decoration and furnishings but that didn't worry Turn. It was always about the foundation. The journey back to the UK was a satisfying one. He thought of his children. It was important for Turn to see what they were doing with their lives, Hope especially. He was yearning to see what the UK was about. He had been away for a while and as he walked through the lobby things seemed to be the same. Good old England. Aaron had come to meet him and stood waiting patiently with Turn's name on a card as though he was a chauffeur.

On the journey back to base, Aaron thought about a few politicians and the way he had to go about opening new centres almost like they didn't want these particular centres to succeed in these areas. They had the community and the businesses in their pockets and they were not going to let them go easily.

Back in the thick of things, Turn chilled and watched from a distance. He listened to what the people at various projects were saying. He listened to the radio, read the news and took the time to hear out anyone who had something to say.

Turn and Aaron were in a large industrial town called Spriloc. Aaron was eager to show Turn their new investment. The only thing holding back the paperwork was the Mayor. He was adamant that the centre would not benefit the people of Spriloc and there were only a few who dared to disagree with him publicly. Turn thought of Hope and her influence as a police chief. She would be a great help right now but he had been unable to contact her and didn't want to ask too many questions or let the guys know how concerned he was. He didn't fret.

After numerous attempts to contact the Mayor at his office, Turn and Aaron decided to just show up. The project had been put on hold until a decision could be made, but everything was in place. Aaron had found some builders who travelled the country for him. Not only did he trust them, they were aware of the layout and just how he wanted the projects to look. Each new structure was better than the last and breathed new hope into the corporation and the people who were involved.

They sat and waited, expecting to see the Mayor at some point during the day. Every so often the secretary announced that he was busy and unable to break his appointments for an adaptation to his schedule. The guys had been waiting for over three hours when a beautiful lady entered the area in which they were waiting. She was about five and a half foot tall with a slender but strong physique, very likely an athlete at some point in her life. Her eyes were grey but the light reflected different colours as it danced around her pupils. Her hair was a mixture of light brown and copper with natural blonde highlights. It had a gentle curl at the end of full waves and was carefully cultivated in a style that showed her lightly tanned clear skin, distributed neatly over an oval-shaped face. A goddess in her own right. She walked with an air of confidence but was able to light up the room with her honest and warm presence. She walked over to where Turn and Aaron were seated, looking over at the secretary as if to make sure she was walking over to the right place. Aaron stood to greet the Mayor's wife, Linda. She politely smiled and offered her hand. She had always encouraged Aaron to persevere with the project in the hope that she could get her husband to see things differently. She couldn't help but look at Turn, she felt full of intrigue and openly looked into his eyes, perhaps lingering for just a second too long. Turn looked at Linda and returned her stare. Aaron introduced Turn to Linda as the project inspiration and founder. Linda didn't need convincing. He put out his hand to meet Linda and gave her a modest but gentle nod as Aaron introduced him to her. Turn's power could be felt instantly and at that point she put everything else to the back of her mind. She was going to make sure that permission for the project was granted. Not only that, she was going to ensure it was a success and anything the guys needed would be provided. Turn had somehow put Linda into a trance without uttering a single word. The secretary politely interrupted. "Sorry, ma'am, the Mayor is available to see you now." Linda excused herself. She was slow to turn around and walked towards the solid broad mahogany doors then she hesitated as she opened them. She looked at Aaron then gave a wink and went in.

The Mayor got up out of his antique, gold-studded, green leather chair to welcome his wife of 32 years into the room. She had been a constant source of strength and support to him, but rarely getting involved in his life. She was faithful and loyal to him and his and he loved her deeply. Mentally, emotionally and physically. They had met at university, each of them from good backgrounds, and they were very career minded. She hadn't changed one bit, she looked exactly the same, a little grey with a few maturing lines but still she looked half her age. Certainly she could pass as one of their children's younger sisters and her grandchildren's aunt. From the first day they met Gregory was hypnotised. Her beauty and skilled hips always had him lusting for more of her sweet wetness. He was a crook but he loved his wife and she knew just how to handle him. They kissed as if their love was brand new. While still in her arms he asked her what he had done to deserve this surprise visit. "I was passing," she replied, "so I thought I'd pop in for a few minutes." She could feel Gregory's erection wilting. If it wasn't for the fact that Aaron and his friends were on her mind, she would be lying on the table, all ready to receive her man, but she knew she had to manipulate the situation.

She casually let go, leaving Gregory full of heat. "I just saw Aaron outside in the waiting area. I thought all that stuff with the project was dealt with. It would be such a good idea and a valuable asset to this town and the people here, why is it taking so long?" Gregory turned and walked back to his chair, this one was difficult to explain to his wife and he did not wish her to think any less of him. If she knew that the only reason he was still in office was because of the bribes and illegal money, he was sure she would leave him.

Gregory was in a tight bind. The large factories based on the outskirts of the town had failed all their inspections and environmental health had declared them as unsafe to work; in fact, a few of the workers were on long-term sick leave, but as nothing had been reported it was just another illness until someone noticed a common occurrence or pattern of the same illness. They were safe but Gregory knew they were running out of time and election time was near. This new centre would only allow the people of Spriloc to alert someone to their fears and create a fight between the government and its people. Gregory was not strong enough to deal with that. Although he had fallen into bad ways he loved his job and his wife always reminded him why he'd wanted to be a mayor. All he had to do now was go back to how it used to be, but he didn't know how with so much greed and unbridled power around him. He would surely lose everything, including his wife. Linda looked at Gregory. She knew this was not going to be easy. He was obviously in it way over his head this time. She moved from the chair and put her fingers on the table, awaiting any signal from Gregory, but his face cowered as he looked down at his shoes. Linda left the room. Aaron and Turn had already left, she was grateful. There was nothing that she could have told them to keep their spirits up. She was going to have to get to the bottom of this.

Aaron and Turn went back to the four-acre piece of land upon which they were hoping to build their new project. Buying the land was easy. No one had any problems in accepting money for waste land that nobody wanted to clean up. It was full of dumped waste, domestic and toxic, and no one knew what else they might find there. The blueprints had been drawn and evaluated, planning permission was all they needed. The town was in need of much restoration, the people were secluded and all of them lived or worked at the factories. It was like being back in time where the people were given enough to live but not enough to challenge themselves.

Aaron's builders were already on site. The clean up was a big job and even though planning permission had not yet been obtained the land was theirs. Removing the waste and household things were one thing but they had to follow strict guidelines in order to remove and dispose of the toxic waste in the appropriate manner. This, of course, was going to cost more. They had already overpaid for the land and every time they were denied planning permission they had to apply yet again and pay even more money. However, money was always at hand. Not only was the business exceedingly prosperous, they even received money through donations from various charities, not forgetting the crew's other extra-curricular activities.

Morgan met Aaron through the project. He and his family became a part of one of the groups when his older son decided that because he didn't like his school he would burn it down. Although not entirely successful, he did succeed in destroying over sixty percent of the building. This resulted in his being expelled and gaining a criminal record all in one go. Morgan felt it was his duty to help with the rebuilding of the school. He had to pay for the criminal damage anyway so, he figured, what was the difference? While enrolling his son, he felt confident in the project. He was sure it would help to guide his son back onto the right path, even if it was only due to the size of Shadow or Flame's theatrics. It wasn't until much later that Morgan, while in conversation with Aaron, had mentioned that he was a builder within his own workforce and that if he ever needed any help he would feel honoured, especially after everything the project had done for him and his family. Aaron didn't even answer him, he pointed to one of the volunteers he knew needed some minor work done on their home, patted his arm and said, "When ya done, come gimme the bill." From then on Morgan and Aaron became firm friends and Morgan could be called upon at any time to rectify any issues pertaining to the centre structure and he and his crew were always happy to travel up and down the country.

T saw Aaron in the distance and waved until Aaron knew it was him. Morgan introduced his head man T to Aaron as even though Morgan was the owner of the company, T was the man that ran the show. He was knowledgeable and, in a word, just like Morgan. Flame and Shadow helped out on most occasions but were not on site today. It soon dawned on Aaron that Turn had never met T; it was a welcome reminder of how much Turn trusted him. Their relationship was a true blessing for him. Before he knew it T was right before him. T was a good man with a humble nature. He shook Aaron's hand and turned to Turn. "My name is T, how are you?" Turn greeted T in similar fashion and started to walk with him around the land. He showed him what could and was to be done before the planning became approved. Turn showed great interest. He had always enjoyed building things and thought of his time in Jamaica, restoring his family home and the 'Blue River' land. They said their goodbyes and Turn walked towards the car. This was what he needed, something he loved and that kept him occupied while he caught up with his children. Maybe he could find Hope and see what was happening in her life. The guys had mentioned that she'd passed by a few times but there didn't appear to be anything out of the ordinary happening for her. She was still on top of her game and hard on the case of the serial killers.

Aaron drove back to headquarters. It was quite a journey as Spriloc was a three-hour drive. They didn't say much on the journey. Turn was thinking about the possibility of working with T on the new project, whilst Aaron was thinking about how to ask T, if Turn could work with him on the new project.

It was late that night when Gregory arrived home in his chauffeur-driven Bentley. He closed the door and watched the driver move slowly up the seventy-foot driveway then stepped towards the entrance. He was startled when he heard a gravel voice approach him from behind the pillar on the porch. It was Judge, he could tell from the smell of the cigar. "Evening, Judge," he said, trying to steady his nerve. Although Judge was a mean and powerful old man his physique resembled that of a nerdy schoolboy. This often humoured Gregory but not tonight. Judge didn't do late night visits unless it was serious.

"Evening, Gregory, I understand you had another visit from that Aaron boy today. I do hope he wasn't given any false hope about his plans of turning this community around?"

"No, sir, he came to the office today but my secretary let him know that I didn't have time for him. He is a persistent little fellow, almost makes me wonder if we should just approve the project, I mean, what harm could it do?"

Gregory did not dare look at the Judge as he immediately knew he had crossed the line. As cool as a January breeze, Judge replied, "I'll tell you what, Gregory, you do that and I'll make sure you go down for everything that is happening in this town and then maybe I could give your wife a little more of the life that she's accustomed to – maybe a lot more. You know what I mean don't you, Gregory?" With that, Gregory walked in, unaware that Linda had been listening from the bedroom window, but brutally aware that Judge did not mince his words. Linda was the best thing that had ever happened to him. He couldn't let anything happen to her.

T called Turn early Monday morning. The call was unexpected but welcome. He asked Turn to work on the project with him and added that Aaron had said a lot of good things about him. He also said his guys were friendly and willing to help if ever he needed it while he was on site. Turn accepted his position and told T he would see him tomorrow.

Turn put down the phone he began to think. He called Hacker and asked him to come around when his day was clear. Turn was staying in one of the project out buildings. Two mini buses had already come and gone since morning, taking different groups to various places, workposts or just trips away. Headquarters had certainly outdone itself; it was a buzzing self-help enterprise that not even Turn could have foreseen.

Hacker got to Turn just after 1pm. He was carrying a case full of complicated electronic devices that didn't make any sense to Turn so he didn't bother to ask. They got straight to it. Turn wanted to know what was happening with Elsa and the kids. He had something in him, niggling away, that made him just want to make sure that they were okay. Hacker was seriously excited; it had been a long time since he had done anything with Turn or the crew. In fact he hadn't done anything since the time he said he was ready for that job where the boy went mad and killed Dead with the chopper knife. He still remembered every part of that night. There was nothing negative in his mind, he understood the purpose and believed in it. It was just traumatic. He was ready to go in and get rid of Dead but he wasn't ready for the other things he saw.

When he and Aaron came back to the UK from Jamaica he didn't really know what to do with himself. He wanted Turn around him, he needed his presence, it gave him a feeling of security. He felt useless. He was given so much: a life, a beachfront home, a family and he didn't have anything to give in return. Aaron coaxed him into teaching at the project. At first it was basic things like how to use a computer. Then he progressed to programming and maintenance, eventually obtaining his teaching certificates. This enabled him to grade the users who had enrolled on the course, awarding NVQs and BTecs. Many of the project clients were able to use their new skills in their job interviews. Some used it to dazzle their children and the courses he provided became very popular. Hacker had really grown up, nothing could have prepared him for his manhood. He was so conscious of it and really hated it when Aaron teased him and said that all he needed now was a wife and three children then he'd wake up in a sweat, before reaching over and tapping the other side of his double bed just to make sure that it was only a dream. A wife and three kids were so far in the future for Hacker he couldn't even imagine it.

They got down to it. Without any visual aids, Hacker was able to tell Turn about his children and Elsa. Turn was especially concerned about Hope. Aaron hadn't said anything about her visiting the centre lately and there was nothing on the news or in the papers about the Chief of Police. Hacker told Turn about how Jason went off the rails, he was the youngest. Jason was always very boisterous. He was in and out of court with charges from arson to grievous bodily harm. Elsa was at her wit's end, not knowing what to do with her baby. Although he was a grown man now, he was still her little soldier. She let go, showing empathy and compassion, but didn't try to understand it anymore. It was at this point Jason knew he had broken his mother's heart. After various punishments, community service, probation, anger management and so on, Jason was finally placed in a minimum security prison where he was to serve a year without parole. However, he was lucky in that he had a sympathetic judge, who took all his previous history into consideration. Not many would have done that. Turn felt truly responsible for the actions of his son and the deterioration of his family. Even though he had left them a long time ago and never thought about the implications of his absence, he didn't realise what devastation could come from him being the man he was. He couldn't change that. This was who he was. The other children had continued in their lives with the support of their own families, including Ian Junior who was a schoolteacher with prospects of becoming a principal.

Turn drove to work the next morning and arrived early. T was impressed. He liked reliability and the strength of a man's word. He had built up his company from hard work, a lot of sweat and trust. Tashma Building Contractors were well known and highly recommended by all who had dealings with them. T introduced his workforce to Turn and told him he would be working with Rohan and Aleck. They didn't hesitate to put Turn in the mix. They were clearing the domestic waste, mainly rubbish bags and odd bits of trash, along with the cookers and rusted zinc baths. It was obvious this was the local dump site, no one to ask any questions and no fines to pay.

Turn stepped into the job like he'd been doing it all his life. He had never been scared of hard work. Rohan and Aleck treated him like an old friend. He watched how the crew worked together. They were tight. They reminded him of the times he and his ghetto brothers were on a job. He liked the way everyone knew when and where they should be without asking. The land was going to be clear before they knew it. He only hoped the planning permission would not get in the way of their progress.

There were banners and flyers everywhere. The election was just two weeks away and the only contender was Gregory. On one side of the town, people just couldn't be bothered to vote and on the other side were those who just didn't want to vote for Gregory. This being the case Hacker found it quite bizarre that over fifty percent of the resident's names were listed as having voted for Gregory in the last two elections, especially as nine of them had died after Gregory's first election but still made the effort to come back from their resting place and vote for him again. This was standard issue fraud, government style. Something needed to be done before the next election took place. Hacker informed Turn of his findings and they both set about devising a plan.

Turn admired T's determination and stamina, there were not many men born in England that Turn had ever looked up to, they shared the same charisma. Turn always felt that children born in England were over privileged and never had to work for anything so when it was time for them to go out into the world and fend for themselves, many were unable to do so. He saw it over and over again, especially with the young teens coming into the project for the first time, some voluntarily others ordered by the courts. It took a few weeks, sometimes months, but they would soon see that they would have to work their way out of their bad habits, to create a new resolution and fight to stand by it using whatever knowledge and will they had. This type of teaching was what made the projects so successful and obviously they had the resources to provide the facilities needed to perform such a task.

The case for Hope was running cold. There were fewer killings and nothing could be linked. No evidence and no two jobs were performed in the same way. The only thing that made her know it was the same serial killer was the information that they had discovered about the victim, almost as if someone had left it there on purpose. Nevertheless, she continued her search. She was starting to think about these vigilantes differently. After seeing what these people had done to others, she was glad they were dead.

T spoke a lot while he was on site. He had aspired to become the man he was by simply remembering where he came from, the root of his success. Some people were privileged enough to be born into a future, the rest they had to work for. T had been in Spriloc since the day he and Aaron went to visit the site, before the land was even bought. He lodged in a small off-road motel. T was a community man who always got to know his surroundings. This was a kind of security thing for him. Knowing where, who and what helped him in all sorts of ways, especially in the job. It was this attitude that provided him with the opportunity of meeting Gregory. He didn't know who he was at first and Gregory sure didn't introduce himself as the Mayor. There was a lake that ran through the forest. Gregory was sitting contemplating as usual when T lost his step and stumbled down the bank. Gregory gave T a hand and helped him on the bench. They laughed. After that, they frequently met at that same spot, just to talk about life and how it comes about. T liked Gregory and Gregory liked T. In fact, when T found out that Gregory was Mayor, by chance, Gregory asked him if he still liked him. It was then that T felt that Gregory had something to hide. Admittedly, they never delved into each other's private affairs, but Gregory almost looked ashamed when it came to light he was the Mayor of a town like Spriloc. T didn't make much of it until Gregory spilt the beans about Judge and his mob connections. The way he spoke could have put the fear of God into most men but it only served to make T realise why a town as big as this was not thriving. Occasionally, top of the range cars would come into town, stop at a few places and leave.

Judge had a lot more than just mob connections. He was running an illegal experiment with a few out-of-state professors. They paid him to get volunteers and the perfect place for those was Spriloc. Due to the desperation and hunger of these people Judge didn't find it hard to get people. The company paid him a thousand pounds for each one. He paid them one pound for every injection they received, which could be anything from 1 to 20 depending on how long their body could withstand the experimental drugs. The company paid Judge ten thousand pounds for every volunteer that died and for the disposal of the body, as some kind of compensation to the family. Judge sent the family a message with a hundred pounds saying their loved one wouldn't be back, burnt the body in an incinerator and threw away the ashes. The ones he couldn't burn he just threw away. He hadn't been caught yet and in a destitute town like Spriloc he believed he never would be. He was a heartless man, driven by money, and he wouldn't let anything get in the way of that.

Shadow, Flame and Turn were having a late lunch in the diner. It was rare that they had lunch but they had things to discuss. Spriloc didn't have much to offer, one clothes store, one café, one news shop. It was very quiet although Flame said this was the sweetest apple crumble he had tasted in a long time. Turn knew something was wrong when he put the fork back down without removing the crumble. Flame had spotted Gregory being hassled by a man in a big black Mercedes. Shadow stopped Turn from going outside and intervening. Gregory picked himself up off the floor and dusted himself down, his face as white as the shirt on his back.

He walked away from the scene without looking back, making sure he dodged just about anything and everything. Aaron and T were on their way to the diner. They had missed the action but could tell that the man walking away was Gregory. T was a little concerned, but decided he would catch up with Gregory later. They walked in and Aaron asked the guys if they had seen what had happened. Flame replied, "Yeh, mon, a Gregory dat." In a nonchalant manor, Turn asked what was going on. T wasn't quick to answer but he felt he knew these people and where they were from. They weren't the average Joes where it was like you were chatting about other people behind their back. It was like telling your brother and finding a solution in the open. T told Turn what he knew about Gregory, telling him about the mob connections and the intermittent arrivals of big money men in their suits and shades. Aaron had quickly caught on that the approval for the project had been a result of whatever these men wanted from Gregory. Turn's first thought was to kill everybody but judging by what T was saying Gregory didn't deserve to die, he was being squeezed and he had to find out why and by whom.

Hope had got word that some big mobsters were coming into the UK. Although they were not wanted, it was always good to keep an eye on them, track what they were doing, who they were seeing and why they were here. Shadow had recognised an undercover officer around the town. There was nowhere to hide so they did their best to blend in which meant more time amusing themselves. He informed the others and they made sure they didn't intervene in anyway. They didn't want to get caught up in the police watch.

It had been days since T had seen Gregory. He sat on the bench day after day waiting for him. As he walked back to his motel one night, he saw a man hovering around the back dressed in ragged clothes and a big hat. T told the man to stay there and he would let him in through the back window. Gregory came through the gap with a thump. He was at his lowest point, looking rough and destitute. He cried and paced around the room, up and down, backwards and forwards. Then he raised his arms and said, "T, they have Linda, I told Judge that I didn't care anymore. They can do what they want to me, I wouldn't continue to have the people of Spriloc live like this anymore. What am I going to do?" T felt somewhat responsible. He had always goaded Gregory on, encouraging him to stand up for what he wanted, to believe in himself and what he stood for.

T paced with him for a while and then stopped. "Things will work out, what I want you to do is go home, clean up and be a mayor. Start the ball rolling, changes have to start somewhere, let them begin with you. Gregory, I will help you, it's difficult to expect things could and will get better, but they will, try not to worry." With that, Gregory stopped pacing and headed for the door. He looked back at T. Although they hadn't known each other long, he knew he could trust him. He wiped his face, fixed his rags as best he could and walked out the door with his head high.

T was due back on site. He sat with his head spinning. He wanted so much to help Gregory but he knew this whole thing was bigger than he could ever have imagined. He kept thinking of Turn. He didn't know why, but he felt if anybody could be the man to help it was Turn. Turn was a humble soul on site but something in his eyes said he was not a man to trifle with. T picked up his hard hat and keys and headed back to the site. Shadow was at the gate, helping the rubbishmen with the load. As he put up his hand to say hello, Shadow grinned with his white teeth and raised his head as if to hail him. Turn was in the deepest part of the dump. It was a steep slide, all nine feet of it. He was pushing a larder freezer, while the men at the top were heaving it up with a rope. T tried to walk down with as much composure as possible but most men ended up at his side at the very bottom and of course a few seconds later the hard hat would join him. The guys at the top of the dig out would always laugh no matter who was next to miss a grip and slide down – work ethics, laugh at everyone.

Turn finished pushing the larder to a point where the guys hauling it up could manage on their own. He came down backwards and turned to greet T. "Wharphen, T, how yuh do."

T smiled, always impressed by the smallest of things. "Turn, me need some advice, we cyan talk?" Turn knew where T was going with this request. He had no problem with helping out but he didn't want T to know that he had anything to do with the resolution. Information was something T was not short of. He told Turn everything Gregory had told him, including his own suspicions. T thought that they were holding Linda in the warehouse at the back of the linen factory. It was not as dirty as the other factories and even though Judge's people were the lowest of scum, they were accustomed to the good life. Messing up their tailored suits for something so petty was not an option.

Turn updated the guys. Aaron was told the bare minimum as usual and the guys made it look like they were always around. This was so that when the heat was on, their alibis were tight. Turn's first visit was to Gregory. He put on his Ninja uniform, including the headpiece, and entered the office. Gregory tended to stay as late as he could in the office since Linda was not at home and Judge had him exactly where he wanted him. What else could he do? He wasn't afraid when he saw the figure walk through the door, he was relieved. Either this man was here to help him or kill him; either way didn't seem like a bad thing right now. Shyly, he stood and greeted the figure dressed as a Ninja.

"Tell me everything," said Turn. Gregory knew help was here. He started at the beginning, making it easy to follow, and didn't miss a thing. By the time he'd finished, Turn knew what he had to do. Judge was a bad man but he was being pushed by the same connections he talked about as being his own guard dogs.

The warehouse was lit up like it was bonfire night. Smoke was coming from the air outlets and there was talk and laughter coming from all directions. Turn couldn't tell how many people were in there but it was definitely rowdy. Linda had to be in there somewhere but he couldn't figure out where. He switched the button, his goggles to infrared, and scanned the warehouse again. There were about 12 men in the front with lots of women dancing around them. They were obviously having a good time. He wasn't able to see through the partition wall that divided the warehouse, he would have to move in closer. He weaved through the Bentleys and Rolls Royces, attaching a small magnetic-looking button to each one, another Hacker speciality. The magnet was small but powerful. It fed off the car's battery like a leech, bleeding its power dry and when there was nothing left to drain it would simply fall off exhausted. Turn didn't need any followers. If this all went wrong he had to make sure there was no way of them catching up with him. He kept the goggles on. He still couldn't see Linda as he circled the warehouse. He was going to have to go in – but why disturb the party? As Turn got closer he became aware of the smell of expensive cigars. They were having a ball. The warehouse was built on stilts so it was above ground level. Turn felt this to be the best way in as from there he could see and hear who was in each room. Bang. Gun shot. Laughing. Linda. What was happening? Turn moved slowly and watched through the infrared as they mocked someone. They fired the gun again. It was like target practice but of course, the target wasn't happy. These guys were rough, they had no scruples, it reminded Turn of Jamaica. The shots continued as Turn moved on. He saw Judge. He was speaking humbly to what must have been the mob leader. Although they both sat with their cigars and spoke like a couple of men in a bar, there was dislike and tension in the air. Judge told Boss what he wanted to do to Gregory; twist his knee, break his legs, rip off his arms. He stood and really took control of the conversation. He was in hot water, somebody had to take his place and the only person viable was Gregory. He was going to be the one to take the blame.

Boss wanted his job done no matter what the cost. He made his intentions clear from the beginning, he was assured by a greedy Judge that Spriloc could be used to store and ship his drugs. That was all that interested him. Whoever was stepping on Judge's toes was not his problem. Boss knew the type of person Judge was. He was a big talker but when it came down to it he wasn't the one. As soon as it became a little hot he started to melt. Boss had to watch Judge real close. With all the money coming in and going out of this town, Boss expected to see a town full of life, flourishing with ambition and interests that engaged the senses. On his trips he often wondered what Judge had done with all the money he had been given for this agreement. He was a swine all right. Boss had no idea what the Judge was up to, so when he turned up with Linda he asked no questions. Judge put her into a room and shut the door. Her cries were heard by all the men at the warehouse and a few wanted to stop it. But Boss put up his cane and said, "We have nothing to do with this, Judge is our host and this is his business." The guys reluctantly backed down.

Turn wanted to kill them both there and then when he heard someone groaning a little further along. It was Linda. She was lying on the floor tied up, clothes ripped, face full of bruises and one eye closed. Turn remembered how she looked the first day he saw her. Now she was hardly recognisable. He felt a twitch in his heart. He wanted to comfort her. She was caught up in something because of her good heart and clear conscience. That wasn't fair. There was no time for emotions. Turn cut through the floor with a small blade to find the floor was damp and rotten, making it easy to get through. Linda didn't utter a word and allowed Turn to take her out of the warehouse. He took her back to the motel where T was staying then placed her in the room and laid her down. He gathered some ice from the box and placed it in a towel over her face. Turn couldn't help but be attracted to Linda. He was feeling things he hadn't felt in a long time. Elsa was his last love and he didn't believe he would ever feel love again. He wasn't a man to show any emotion. He gave his all – in his work or for someone else – but when it came down to expressing how he felt for someone even he had a hard time working out exactly what he was feeling.

Linda didn't know who was helping her but she was grateful. She was unable to see through her swollen eyes, but the ice on her face started to numb the pain. She reached out and caught Turn's arm, rubbed his bicep and covered his hand with hers. Turn wanted to touch her but he had to finish what he had started and return her to her rightful place. He shut the door behind him then, as he passed T's lodge, he noticed the television was on. He looked in through the window to see T was snoring in front of the screen. Turn took a few steps towards the exit. He stopped and walked back to Linda's room then entered with ease. Linda turned in the bed and sat up. She was not frightened, she knew it was her rescuer, she could feel him. Turn walked towards Linda's bruised and swollen face. The pull that she had on him was too strong. He couldn't deny himself this one desire. He sat on the bed facing her. They leant together as though they knew what was going to happen and kissed. Although her lips were cut and sore, she could hardly feel the pain through the kiss. Exasperated by the encounter yet breathless from its harmony, Turn left the motel without a word.

The warehouse was buzzing. Judge was in the middle of all the noise, raising his voice, telling the others how worthless they were, asking how they could have failed to see or hear Linda escaping. He was going on and on and on. Turn just kissed his teeth – what a fool. Judge was definitely playing the big man now; maybe he thought this would help him with Boss and his own plans for him. Boss sat and watched with a sense of coolness. Judge was going a bit too far now but he would let him continue. Pussy, thought Boss. Although the town had provided him with everything he needed for the buying, storing and supplying of his drugs, Judge was a man on the edge. He was losing his cool, getting caught up and feeling like he would have to make alternative arrangements.

Flame had been keeping track of what was happening. He was way up in the trees, looking through the infrared binoculars, his earpiece connected to a sound tracker. He could hear the vexation as they tried to drive away when they found out that Linda was missing. A few of the guys reluctantly went into the forest in their expensive shoes, cussing Judge with every step. When he saw Turn re-appear, he radioed down to him. Apparently, now that Judge had lost Linda he had nothing to plea bargain with. He felt that Gregory was becoming too strong and wasn't easily swayed anymore. He needed Linda to keep things running the way he wanted, he needed this money from Boss, he depended upon it. It turned out that Judge was in way over his head. He hadn't lost anything yet but his reputation and this next pay off would put him back right among the big players. Nobody took him seriously, he was a social dwarf and his rancid mouth didn't help him, in fact it only got people's backs up. But somehow he always managed to stay on top with his big man mentality, saying how he'd take anyone down. He didn't need bodyguards for that. As Turn watched from the back, he and Flame agreed that Judge seemed to be digging his own hole. They left the scene and went back to base. Turn told Shadow to go check on Linda. Let T find her, Gregory would be relieved to know his wife was alive.

At work T and Turn were talking. T was telling Turn how he and Shadow found Linda in the lodge next to his. He couldn't believe it. He said that he called Gregory straight away to come and get her as by the looks of her she sure was lucky to be alive. Turn told T that he should tell his friend that he was lucky this time. He needed to turn things around with his people and make Spriloc the place it should be. Although T didn't know Turn had anything to do with it, he knew by speaking to him that something good would come of the situation. He made sure he told Gregory everything Turn had said, adding a few things here and there. Gregory had definitely had a change of heart. He was a man on a mission. His heart bled when he saw Linda but that didn't stop him. Gregory had plans for his town and even if he was going to be the one hanged for the things that had happened, he would tell the whole story with his head held high.

Turn, Shadow and Flame were waiting for the dump trucks to arrive. Flame asked Turn what would happen now. Shadow stood and said, "The way things are going, Judge will get wiped out by someone else."

"I'm not so sure," said Turn, "he has obviously created a lot of enemies but Boss showed no intention of getting wrapped up with Judge any more than he was already. In fact it seemed like Boss was getting ready to ship out." Judge was going to mess up at some point, all three of them were sure of it.

Aaron entered Gregory's office, a few minutes early for his appointment. He didn't want to miss anything. The secretary was welcoming as before and showed Aaron right in. Gregory smiled as Aaron entered and showed him to the chair in front of his desk. There was a moment's silence. "Aaron," said Gregory, "I want you to start at the beginning, tell me about this project, tell me everything you want to do for my town." Aaron didn't hesitate, he told Gregory more than he had asked for, he was on a roll. Gregory had already signed the papers for the release of the plans but he was glad to hear just what the future of Spriloc had for it. At the end of Aaron's mega presentation, Gregory stood while Aaron sat in anticipation. Gregory took out the planning permission and handed it to Aaron. The two of them were delighted. They shook hands firmly and smiled. Gregory said farewell and saw Aaron out the door. He went back to his desk and sat down. Not even the thought of Judge's disapproval could change how good he felt at the moment. Aaron went straight back to the site, unable to hold back the grin or excitement. He blew his horn, came to an abrupt stop, stood on his car bonnet and announced the news. The guys cheered and a parade of hard hats was thrown into the sky.

T was on a mission. Things were all ready to go, materials were already on site, or was on the way. The last of the rubbish had gone and the rest of the cement was about to go down to finish the rudiments. It was getting dark and the guys knew this would be it for the day. They cleaned up and headed for a late dinner at the diner. Sharon the waitress was sure to fix them up proper.

Judge looked out of his window and down at the open area which was soon to be the project. He had told Gregory he would make sure his time in office was over, but Gregory didn't fluff and he didn't like that. Boss was not sending any more drugs, he was moving what had been stored. He had told Judge that the agreement wasn't going to work out anymore and as long as his last transactions went by smoothly he would get his money and a bonus. Judge was happy with that, he knew not to mess with Boss anyway. Although he tried to hide it, he was scared of him.

Morning had come. The guys got on site as early as possible making sure they used as much of the sunlight as possible. When they arrived, they noticed a lot of extra tracks from what looked like truck wheels. They were too big to have been left by a car. The guys thought nothing of it as the delivery men usually dropped off the first load of materials before dawn. T walked down into the pit first. There was an awful smell. Aaron thought it was the drains but the guys knew what it was. As they walked further into the pit, they began to notice flies everywhere. T dropped to his knees when he saw the bodies; lifeless, swollen and rotten. He begged the others to go back. Shadow held on to Aaron, advising him not to go and when he didn't listen, he told him he wasn't going. Turn and Flame headed back to Aaron's car. Turning it slowly away from the site they drove to the lodge and prepared for battle. This was the work of Judge and nobody could have told him any different.

Judge lived in a four-floor detached townhouse with swimming pool, sauna, walk-in wardrobes; a life of luxury. He sat counting his money, cash spread across the table. As promised, Boss had given Judge the extra bonus. Flame scaled the wall to the second floor, while Turn entered via the cellar window. Judge had no family and no pets, he lived for himself and no one else. Flame stood for what seemed like forever at the doorway, watching Judge count his money. The only reason he looked up was because a fifty pound note floated off the table. Startled, he asked who Flame was as he swiped the money off the table and into a bag. "Na worry ova meh, wharphen to you?" Judge picked up the bag and ran for the stairs, not seeing Turn coming up as he was going down. Turn unleashed his sword and slit his belly open with one swing, just enough to let his intestines fall out into his hands as he continued down the stairs. Judge collapsed onto his chair, pleading with Turn to leave him alone. He could have some of the money in the bag if he would just leave him. He started to feel sick at the sight of his intestines sprawled out over his lap. Turn decided to do the speech thing. He wasn't going anywhere and he had a few things he felt Judge should listen to before going to the gates. Flame was rummaging about upstairs looking through all the loose papers. He noticed a contract. It was between the professors and Judge, stating what the experiment was and how much each volunteer was to get under the different circumstances. There was a small piece on the bottom that Judge had to sign and pass on to the volunteer's next of kin. Flame brought it downstairs and showed it to Turn who tutted as he read it. Judge knew what it was and thought he had burnt it.

"Judge, before I continue to kill you, I want you to sign this paper. You always stated you had guts, now you've got plenty. Sign the papers."

Judge, feeling drowsy and in agony, signed the contract without leaving any blood on the paper. Flame rolled up the contract and put it in his inner sleeve. They walked to the door, Judge cursing them out. "You can't leave me like this."

"You're right," said Turn. He walked back to Judge and stabbed him with one of the syringes he had found in the cellar. It was marked 'type O'. Then he picked up the bag of money and they left.

It took two months to complete the building with the police and press all over the site because of the dead bodies. The autopsies revealed that they had a deadly form of rat poison in them and the professors stated that this helped with eternal youth and flexibility. Turn had given a lot of the money away to the people of Spriloc. The rest was left from Judge as a donation to the charity.

Many of the people didn't have any skills and wouldn't know what to do with the money that he had left them; the project would be able to teach them everything they needed to know and more.

Gregory was voted mayor again – he had no competition – but he swore he would make the town one of the best in the state and with Linda by his side Turn didn't doubt that for a minute. He didn't say goodbye, he just raised his hand and drove away.

9

Aaron and Turn did a tour of all the centres. Things were fine, Aaron had everything under control. On his return to the main office, he found Hope waiting in the library listening to the storyteller. She jumped up when she saw Turn then poked him and said, "You never returned any of my calls, where have you been?"

He held his hands up as though he was under arrest and explained that he had just got back from Jamaica. They sat in the office while he told her it was a mixture of business and pleasure plus he and the crew needed a break. She went on to say she had never been to the Caribbean before. She had always dreamed of it and knew she was born in the West Indies and came here when she was really young, but had never talked about it. She frowned as though she had just remembered something but went on. After her father died she didn't have any family left over there so she never bothered to go. She wanted to but there was no reason, her life was set. Turn let her know that anytime she wanted to go and use one of the cottages she was more than welcome. It would be a good experience for her and the children. She sat back with a smile as she thought about taking the kids out there. As usual she was really delighted to see him. After a few hours she looked at the time and realised that she was late for a meeting regarding repeat offenders. She briefly went into a case, which was the main reason for the meeting. "It's happening about 100 miles up north," she explained to Turn. "A lot of young girls are being kidnapped, raped and killed. There are lots of sick people out there." With that she got up and gave Turn a kiss on the cheek. "Take care of you," she added, "speak soon." Turn wondered if she had ever thought about the fact that they had shared a plane together from the same country in which they were investigating similar murders. He often did. Turn's mind wandered back to the kidnapped girls Hope was speaking off. He could smell death but maybe it was a trap. He would lay low with that one and deal with the others just in case, it would be a shame to get caught over something so simple.

It was a normal day with the guys scouting the streets looking for suspects. The shopping centre was more crowded than usual. There in the middle of centre was a middle-aged woman. She was spinning around in circles, acting demented and crying uncontrollably. Shadow stopped her from spinning, held her arms and looked into her eyes. He could feel her pain as he put her head on his broad chest but finally she started to relax.

She spoke softly like a mouse. She told them that her daughter had been kidnapped and the police had slowed the search because they all believed that she was dead as it had been over two months since she first disappeared. The guys had had a few cases like these, letters giving dates and approximate times their little girl had been taken. It was difficult to come up with one suspect. Hacker put pin points on the big screen to show where and when the child had been taken. When he enlarged the area of the image it showed an inward spiral. Maybe they would be able to catch the serial killer as he was making his move. All they had to do was follow the dots. The killer or killers were very careful about how they committed the crime. They left no clues and made sure they were never seen. There was nothing to go on, except this inward spiral.

10

Greg brought the mail to Elsa. As he walked into the room he was waving a letter in the air. "I think we should open this one first," he said, "its postmark says Jamaica, it says it's for Hope Baxter but in care of you." Elsa reached out, slightly bemused, it had been a long time since she had received a letter from Jamaica. It looked very formal. Elsa looked at it carefully, wondering what it may contain, unsure as to whether she should open it or not. She laid it gently on the bedside table and reached for the telephone.

Hope had just shut the front door when she heard the phone ringing. "Mum, Gran's on the phone." Hope picked up the line in the hallway so she could collapse on the stairs at the same time.

"Hey, Mumsy, how are you?" They spoke about things in general for a while until Elsa mentioned the letter. Hope had no idea who it could be from, she urged Elsa to open it. Elsa described the letter in detail as she pulled it out of the envelope.

"It's from a solicitors," she said, "it says that they are writing to advise you that after the unfortunate death of Cyril and Beverley Shepheard, you have been invited to attend the reading of their last will and testament."

"Are you sure that letter is for me?" Hope's mind started twitching. She remembered telling Turn some time ago that she would love to go to the West Indies, here was her chance. Elsa explained who Cyril and Beverley were. She knew that after the trauma that Hope had undergone, she wouldn't remember a thing.

Hope booked the flights and began to look for accommodation. She thought of Turn's offer and called the project. Aaron answered the phone in haste, he was eating pizza, writing a report and making notes about an idea he'd had, so the phone ringing caught him offguard. As usual Turn was not around so Hope asked Aaron if it was possible, as she needed to make plans as soon as she could. Aaron saw no problem in allowing Hope to stay in one of the houses for a week and called ahead to let Zinc know she was coming.

Hope was on a plane the next day, anxious, tense but happy. She had left the children with Elsa for the week and was looking forward to some free time on the beach. The Blue River car and chauffeur picked her up from the airport, graciously welcoming her to Jamaica. When they pulled up to the house, Hope stayed in the car as she thought the driver was collecting somebody else or dropping something off. She looked out of the window at the waterfront but didn't see the driver taking her luggage out of the boot and placing it into the open hallway of the house. It was Zinc that opened the car door, extended his hand and introduced himself to Hope. Hope was escorted out of the car and up the steps to the front door. He showed her where everything was and informed her that she would have her own housemaid. If she needed anything else she was to let him know. Hope didn't say a word. She was still amazed at the beauty of the house and the people she'd had the pleasure of meeting. Zinc explained that he had already arranged for the car to take her to her appointment at the solicitors the following afternoon but if at any time she wanted the use of the car and chauffeur all she had to do was call. Hope reached inside her purse and took out some money as a tip but Zinc touched the top of her hand and said, "That won't be needed here, ma'am. Enjoy your stay. Good day."

Hope was in wonderland. She spun around on the marble floors and looked up at the crystal chandelier. It was beautiful. After a superb dinner, Hope went up to her room where she found the extra wide patio doors were open. It made it seem like she was on the beach as she could hear the water rolling in and out as she closed her eyes. Finally, she fell asleep amid the sound of the gentle breeze.

Hope had overslept. It was midday when she first arose. She looked at her watch and thought about her clothes crushed in the suitcase. She had been too tired to think about that last night. She got up and walked towards her bathroom. As she passed the walk-in wardrobe she noticed that her clothes were hung and pressed, shoes in order and shined. Hope smiled, she could get used to the queen treatment. She ran a bath and filled it with bubbles. She wasn't anxious about the reading of the will, she felt it would be nice to know about the people that took in her dad when he had nobody. Lunch consisted of a range of tropical fruits, and the car was on time. What else could a woman want?

The chauffeur took Hope to the swivel doors of the solicitor's office and explained that she wouldn't have to call as he would wait for her in the car park. Hope nodded. The receptionist was very polite and efficient, asking Hope if she wanted a cup of tea or coffee while she waited in the family room for the meeting to take place. Hope refused but said thank you. The family room was well set out, non-invasive, large and welcoming. It was strategically laid out with single chairs, sofas, and coffee tables. All in all it was very calming and the finishing touch was that it had a beautiful view from the window. There were a few people in there already but Hope managed to find a seat opposite the window and waited to be called.

After ten minutes a gentleman entered. He called out in a deep voice, "Would the people here for the reading of the will of Cyril and Beverley Shepheard please follow me into the reading room." Hope got up slowly and analysed the room. There didn't appear to be anyone else but her waiting. *How strange* she thought, she had travelled all the way from England to be here and wondered if anybody else had tried. She followed the gentleman to the reading room. The solicitor stood up as Hope walked towards him, they shook hands and she introduced herself to him. He welcomed her to the country and was delighted that she had made the journey. He sat back down and opened up his folder. Just then the door swung open and in stepped a man who stated he was Antoine Shepheard. He was panting. The solicitor stood again, greeted Antoine and pointed to a seat. "Please, catch your breath, we are just beginning." Hope smiled at the man, he smiled back but nothing was said. The solicitor started to read the will. When he announced that Hope was to get the house, land and its contents, she gasped. Antoine looked at her and asked the solicitor who she was. Silently, she looked at Antoine with a tear in her eye. The solicitor continued. The rest of the children, including Antoine, were left with everything else – including the house in America, bonds and any shares they may have. With that the solicitor asked Hope and Antoine to sign a form to acknowledge that they had been present at the reading and understood what had been said to them. Hope was handed the deeds and keys to the property while Antoine was told the amount that would be shared equally between him, his brothers and sisters. When Antoine was told how much money he would get he smiled. It was obvious that's all he wanted. Hope stood up, thanked the solicitor and wished Antoine the all best. She left the office, got into the car then asked the driver to leave. A smooth drive usually relaxed her and she needed to clear her head. From what her mum had explained, Cyril and Beverley were from America, they had taken her dad Ian Baxter in when things got rough for him. They welcomed him in and before long he was like a son to them, he was family. She explained that Hope was born there and Beverley doted on her. Elsa told her she would write occasionally and send pictures of the kids to them. She didn't know anything else and she definitely wouldn't know why she was left the house.

They had been driving for two hours and Hope finally gave the chauffeur the address. They were already on that side of the island and within 15 minutes the driver started looking for door numbers. Hope felt good when she saw the house: it was beautiful. She asked the driver if he would come with her. He didn't hesitate. There was a barrel with some fresh, ready-to-plant flowers. A gardener appeared from behind the bush, he was humble and polite. He apologised for being there without permission and went on to say that he just loved the garden at the house. He added that Cyril and Beverley were like his brother and sister, they had fed and clothed his family. He walked away when the water filled his eyes. Hope was touched. As they walked up the path she was strangely drawn towards the outhouse but went into the house first, the house was at peace. So clean and cared for. She walked through the house and looked at the pictures, spotting one of her with her brothers and sisters. She smiled. The driver always made sure he didn't say anything but as he walked around the house behind Hope he couldn't hold back his praise for its design and layout; he was really impressed. Hope looked through the drawers in the bedroom; they were still filled with Cyril and Beverley's belongings. She didn't want to pry but couldn't see any other way to deal with it. What was she going do with all these clothes and keepsakes? Surely their children would have wanted something to have that was theirs. The house was so big, how could the two of them have coped in here all by themselves? They were nearing the end of the journey around the house and when it was time to leave they made sure everything was locked. She called the solicitors' office and asked them to pass on a message to Antoine Shepheard for him to call her regarding his parent's belongings. She put the phone away and looked up. There in front of them was the outhouse.

It was like an annexe, small and delightful. The door opened with ease. Immediately, a visitor would find him or herself in a very large room. It resembled a studio flat. The bed, kitchenette, tables and chairs were all in the room, the only other door was to a small bathroom. It was so cosy. The bedspread was hand sewn and there were little hand-picked flowers in the vases. Although they were starting to droop they gave the room a smell that emphasised its cleanliness. Everything was in its place, including a beautiful rocking chair. Hope sat in the chair and let her eyes wander around the room. She felt so comfortable. She rocked for a while and watched the driver looking at some pictures on the far wall. Hope went over, she hadn't seen these pictures before. There was a beautiful lady in most of them including one in which she was heavily pregnant and then holding her new born child. Hope gave out a 'aghh'.

The driver looked at her and then back at the picture. "Ya know, you look just like her. If I didn't know better I would have said it was you." Hope looked at him. With the realisation that this could really be her mother, she inspected the pictures over and over again getting more and more excited. She carried on along the wall and in most of the pictures saw a man standing alone. In a few he would be holding the baby or in a group picture with what must have been Cyril and Beverley. Could this be her dad? She thought he looked familiar but didn't dwell on it too much. Things can look any way you want if you want it badly enough.

She looked back at the picture of the man with Cyril and Beverley. He looked about 15 but that's not what most caught Hope's attention. It was the fact that this man looked like her little brother. It had to be her dad, it just had to be. She pulled the picture from the wall and there in clear ink was written *Ian, Cyril and Beverley*. She took the others from the wall. *Clarisa, Hope and Ian*. She couldn't believe she had found these. She kept looking along the wall; the pictures showed stages of Ian getting older and older. As he got older Hope felt closer and closer to him. She held the pictures to her chest. She removed all the pictures from the outhouse, took one more look around and carefully eased up the door. Hope got back to the house and sat at the table. The housemaid made her a drink and asked if she would like something to eat. Hope looked up and said, "No, thank you." She spread the pictures out across the table and looked at each one carefully. She knew this was her mum and dad in the picture and she felt fortunate to have found them, but there was something about this man Ian Baxter. She fell asleep with her head on the table.

Morning came and she was gently woken by Zinc and the sweet smell of Blue Mountain's very own coffee. She wiped her eyes. "Hmmm, thank you, I must have dozed off. Zinc commented on her trip, pointing to the picture. He asked how she knew Turn.

"Turn?" she replied.

"Yes, I mean, these pictures are quite old but that's definitely Turn. He's a great man, he holds his word and he's faithful, he owns this Blue River complex. He took me from the streets with my family and gave me a home and a big job."

It was all making sense to her. *Did he know? Had he planned this? He's alive!* She thought of the time they came back from America together. *Why was he really there?* The note that was left with the file on her desk, which contained explicit details regarding the death of her husband and his killer. The things she had told him about certain cases and within a few days the murderer was found dead. Was he the person the entire police force were looking for? It can't be, it's my dad! She needed time to digest it all.

The guys had been carefully tracking the serial kidnapper. With the calculations that they had made, they were sure he had picked his victim already and they already knew where and when. They were hiding out. The police had the same idea as them but they were waiting patiently in another area. They didn't have Hacker on their side. School was out. There were lots of little blonde girls walking towards the gate. Hacker had the CCTV on lock down. Flame tapped Shadow and pointed to a man wearing a wig. He looked suspicious. A split second later the same person walked back to a people carrier. They had two little girls with them; even though they walked by themselves following the man, they kept looking back at the gate as though they were looking for somebody. They got into the carrier and drove off sharply. Hacker tracked the number plate. It was registered in the name of a man called Tony, he had been arrested before for drink driving and transsexual activities in a park. Flame was sure that was the person they were looking for. They followed him slowly, Hacker had him on the tracker so if they lost him it wouldn't be a problem. He drove for miles, almost reaching out of state. The guys were cautious. The man pulled up in front of a little bungalow and went into the garage then before getting out of the carrier he made sure the garage door was fully closed. The guys parked the van around the corner. They approached the bungalow one to the back, one to the front and one on the garage. Shadow gained entry first, through the side window. The front of the house was empty, there was no sound and no alarms. He pulled Flame through the window and let Turn in by the door. They searched the top of the house. There was nothing, the garden was all lawn, all 60 feet of it. To the naked eye there was nothing to be seen. Flame could smell something, a weak smell that seemed to come up from the floor. They looked for a hatch or a hidden door in the garage and sure enough there it was. It was hidden by a shelving unit. They entered slowly, the deeper they went the more they could smell death. The transmitters went out of range and Hacker lost communication. They could hear the killer singing away, he was singing over the crying children.

Hope's head was pounding. The first thing she was going do was see Turn, she was going to show him the pictures and wait for his reaction. The stewardess poured Hope a drink and asked if she was all right. Hope nodded thank you. She tried to relax.

Shadow put up his hand to signal Flame and Turn to stop and drop. The singing had stopped. In the reflection of some broken mirror he could see the killer's bare feet. They slowly moved into the open area. The killer started to sing again but this time there was no crying. The underground washroom had blood splattered across the walls. The smell of rotten flesh seeped through their masks. There were cameras in every corner of the room. The killer stood in the middle of the washroom, he had a stage light above him and was completely naked. He wore only the wig they had seen him in earlier, and he was dripping with blood. He sang and danced in front of metal cages and twisted and turned unaware he was being watched by anyone other than his chosen audience. He had the breasts of a woman and pushed his dick down between his legs so it was not visible from the front. Flame stood still. They had seen a lot of perversion in the time they had been doing this, but this felt like something new. Could it get any worse? Were there people out there who really do this? These cameras were recording something, why would they want to watch this nastiness all over again? Shadow looked at Flame, truly believing that this was his last mission. He couldn't bear to see these things. He understood that he was doing this for the good of his world, but his soul could not bear to be a witness to such things anymore. He said his usual prayer and asked God to forgive him for his sins. Turn could see movement in a few of the cages. He hoped the children were still alive. At that point the killer walked over to a table and picked up a knife. He turned and looked into one of the cameras but didn't notice the guys as they watched him from behind the bright lights. As he approached the cages the children started to cry. He took the knife and started to jab through the holes and rattled the knife along the doors. They were screaming. Flame went to move in, but Turn held him back. He needed to see what this man was really up to.

Hacker was getting concerned. He'd lost contact with the guys nearly an hour ago and didn't think he could hold on any longer. What if they were in trouble? He drove over to the house and saw the van. They must still be here. He parked across the road and checked the police radio. Hacker realised he wasn't the only person watching the house, the police had finally figured out where the man was. They had set up in the house next door and had cameras discreetly located to show the front and back of the house. He pretended he had stopped to look at the map book, had a cigarette and laid his head back, tilting his cap over his eyes as though he was asleep. He had no way of warning the guys without attracting any unwanted attention so he decided to keep a low profile.

Tony took one of the children out of the top cage, it stood about four feet off the ground. He pulled the child out by her hair and she dropped to the ground with a thud, ripping her hair from her scalp. There was an almighty scream which pierced the room and her hands tightly held her head. She was trembling. Tony took the hair and pasted the blood over his lower pubic hair then looked in the mirror and danced, holding it in place to prevent it slipping down. He noticed the little girl trying to crawl past him. She was going towards the lights. He gripped her ankle and swung her round, scraping her body along the floor and smashing her head into the walls as she went round and round then finally she crashed. He let go of her and she flew into a surgeon's table; the table fell over, sending his tools all over the room. He crouched down and picked up the scalpel next to her. She was now in too much pain to cry. He stopped singing and placed the scalpel near her throat then sliced into her skin gently, trying to peel the skin away from her face. The little girl was now unconscious but her body went into a violent seizure, making him rip the skin. He shouted out, "You stupid little bitch!" and stabbed her repeatedly with the scalpel, releasing his aggression. After a few minutes he scooped her back up and pushed her lifeless form back into the cage.

Hacker heard a knock on the car window. He removed his hat and looked up to see a uniformed police officer. He asked him what his business was here and Hacker replied by saying he was resting before his long journey. The police officer asked to see his ID. When he was satisfied that Hacker was who he said he was, he asked him to move on as this area was cordoned off. Hacker agreed and moved his car to the next street. He was sure the police were going to make entry but there was nothing he could do about it. He switched on his satellite and started to look for any live feed that may be transmitting somewhere else. He thought he might catch something from the police cameras but what he found was the images from the cameras in the washroom. He started to record them. He followed the transmissions and found that there were over twenty households watching it live, like an illegal porn station. He couldn't see the guys in any of the shots so he registered the feed reporting the homes that were watching it and forwarded the transmission to the police.

The plane had landed. As they sat in the aircraft waiting for the seatbelt light to be switched off, Hope switched on her mobile phone. She had to get hold of Turn. The network sent a text welcoming her back to the UK and then it rang. It was one of her detectives and he sounded frantic. "Hope, we've found the serial killer, and we're receiving a live transmission showing his every move, it's revolting. Someone is waiting for you in the arrivals lounge, hurry!"

Hope couldn't wait. She took off her belt, grabbed her hand luggage and walked towards the door. As the steward approached her she showed her badge and said, "As soon as these doors open I'm getting off." She didn't wait for her luggage as she could get that sent to her. Hope ran through the foyer, looking for her driver. Before she knew it she was in an unmarked car, being briefed upon their findings, sirens blaring, on her way, dodging traffic.

Turn had seen enough. He signalled the move. They stood up slowly and came from behind the lights into the vision of Tony. Evil had met its match. They circled him and Flame flicked a small blade. Tony hissed and he dodged it, spitting on Flame as he did so. Shadow threw his fist into the back of his spine. He curled up and cried out as he fell to his knees. Shadow, whose fist held the power of ten men, walked over to the cages and opened the doors. Among the children was vermin and bile, they were in a bad way. The cages were overcrowded and they were lying on top of one other. In one cage a little girl lay next to the arms and legs of the body she rested upon, rotting away. Shadow had tears in his eyes, he wept for their souls. He pulled them out one by one and found that for some reason they were not afraid of him.

Tony shouted out, "Leave them, they belong to me, they each have what I need!" They followed Shadow back up the tunnel. He carried those who couldn't walk and prayed for the ones who couldn't hold on any longer. The children were dehydrated, abused, taunted and bewildered. There were 13 little girls, covered in dirt and blood. He put them in the front room where it was warm and empty. He told them it was all over, they would see their families soon and be at home in their warm, clean beds. He went back downstairs and carefully taking them one by one he wrapped the dead children in a sheet and placed them in the bedroom upstairs. Each time, he told the little survivors that the child he was carrying was asleep and on their way to heaven. There were six in all, each of them dead.

Hope was nearby when the detective called her. "You'll never guess who else is down there with the serial killer. Not only the vigilantes, it's incredible, this footage is amazing! We have also worked out that somebody is actually directing the live feed to us, the sergeant isn't as good as he thinks he is. They are even forwarding us the addresses of the people who are watching the live feed as we speak. We have plain clothes officers on the way now. This is huge. The network is getting bigger as well, at first there were just over 20 households watching the sicketts, now there are nearly 50. We are pursuing each one. A couple of these people are on the offenders list already. This is high profile stuff." With that, he hung up. Hope looked at her driver and told him to step on it, she had missed too much already.

Turn asked the killer what he was thinking of, taking people's children and handling them like that. The killer didn't speak, instead he kicked and scratched. This man was real sick but he would get no pity from them. Flame reached for the same scalpel that he had used on the little girl. He walked towards the killer with it held out in front of him. As he did so the killer dashed across the floor until his back hit the wall. Turn was next to him. He shouted, "You'll go to hell if you touch me!" but Turn was in no mood to hear any preaching from someone who could do what he did.

Hope arrived on site and briefly scanned the footage that had been recorded already. She was disgusted. Then she asked one of the tactical officers if they had seen any movement inside. He shook his head, nothing prominent, some swaying of the netting covering the window but, he explained, that could be the result of a draught. "Get closer, we need to make sure," ordered Hope.

Hacker could hear the buzzing from Shadow's radio. It was moving in and out of range so he knew something was happening in there. He just wanted to get to them but didn't know how. With the number of police that were surrounding the building he knew it wasn't going to be possible and there was no way the police were going to let them walk away from this, everyone would know who they were.

They had tortured the man enough, crushing his kneecaps and shoulders, hoping he would repent or beg forgiveness. But he didn't even say sorry. He shouted, "Look what you have done to me, look what you've done to me!"

With that, Turn held his head up against his legs and said, "*You* look." He slit his throat deeply from ear to ear and felt the warmth of his blood trickle through his fingers. It felt good. He stood like that for a moment and let the relief fill his body. He had rid the world of more evil. The assassin lifestyle had worked out for him, he removed the bad and gave back plenty to those who needed it. He moved away from the body, turned to Flame and the two of them gave each other a brotherly hug. They checked the cages to make sure they were empty and walked back up the tunnel. Shadow was in the front room. He was making the girls drink some water from his bottle. The guys had never had to deal with survivors before and now there were 13 of them. Hacker got through to hear the radio echo that there were police everywhere.

"Do you hear me? They are everywhere, there is no way out, they have blocked the back doorway, can you hear me?"

Flame replied, "We have 13 survivors, badly injured, we cannot use them as bait, you gotta think of something." The guys turned to the people carrier in the garage.

Flame added, "Dat nah ga mek it."

"We have no choice," said Turn.

Shadow told the girls to cover their ears. "Someone will be here for you soon and they will bring you home, but we must go now. Don't be afraid." One of the little girls ran to him and held him tight. "You'll be all right, honey, I promise." He placed her with the others and shut the door behind him.

The people carrier smashed through the garage doors and backed straight out onto the main road. They changed gear and sped off with the sounds of sirens following them closely. Some of the other officers stormed the house and found the little girls safely in one room and the others in the bedroom. "You can't wake them, they're on their way to heaven," one of the little girls said.

The car chase was dangerous with Hacker following as best he could without losing them. An overhead helicopter tracked the chase but when the gap between them and the police cars became too great the pilot gave the order to shoot at the tyres. The guys had bullets showered upon them from above. They didn't know where they were driving to, they just needed to get somewhere – anywhere. Flame shot back at the helicopter but as he leaned out of the window a bullet from the police car hit him from behind. He was losing a lot of blood but still shooting. Shadow was hit next as he was driving, the bullet catching him right in the chest causing him to collapse onto the steering wheel and the van to hit the curb and flip over. Turn was shaken but alive. He punched through the back glass and started to run. Bullets were flying and he had been hit. He knew it but kept going, running through the alleys and jumping fences. As he landed he was hit four more times and this time he was laid out on the concrete. He couldn't go any further.

The police radio said 'man down'. Hope was elated over the fact they had caught the vigilantes. Her oldest case was now soon to be closed. Turn was still alive. The officer that got to him first looked at him in amazement. He held on to him, so as to comfort him until the paramedic came. He said, "I know you're not bad and in many ways I look at you as a hero but what you have done is illegal. They won't tolerate it, most of the guys salute you but there are a few who you have put to shame. But we all know your intentions are good, it would be a shame to see a warrior go out like this."

The paramedic arrived with a stretcher and medical kit. They removed his mask and covered his wounds to slow the blood loss and put him on the stretcher. Hope was at the ambulance door; she wanted to see who this man was. As the paramedics came out she started to talk aloud. "At last we've got the vigilantes, you guys have really caused some damage to our justice system. I only hope you realise that the judge…" It was then Hope saw Turn, Ian Baxter, her father lying on the stretcher. She gazed deeply into his eyes. Although her emotions were up and down she managed to hold on to the stretcher.

Hope felt weak and dazed. She bent down to his ear and said, "I love you, Dad." They placed him inside the ambulance.

As the driver closed the door, he looked at Hope. He had heard what she said to Turn. He took her hand, covered it with his and said, "Don't worry, your father is strong, I'm honoured to have been near him." Then he got into the ambulance and sped to the allocated hospital. Hope stood still. Hacker watched from the corner of the alley. He had lost everything he had ever known that was good. Since the first day he met them, they had welcomed him, no questions asked. They had helped him develop his talents and allowed him to grow from a boy to a man. He loved them. He went to see Aaron as he didn't want anybody else to tell him. Hope called Elsa; she needed her now more than ever.

Turn was in intensive care for two weeks after his operations. He was placed in a secure part of the hospital with a guard by his door. When he woke up the guard was standing next to him. He said, "I didn't want you to wake up alone, the world needs more people like you, people who take matters into their own hands." Then he smiled as he walked back into the hallway, alerting the nurses to the fact that Turn was awake.

It wasn't long before the world knew who the

assassin was. The newspapers had it plastered on the front page. Ian Baxter.

Hope had been on an emotional rollercoaster. Everything made sense but she just couldn't grip it. Everyone was dumbstruck. The family were all together at Elsa's. They cried, they shouted, they hugged, they blamed, they wanted their dad and more than anything Elsa wanted her soul mate.

When the guard at the hospital called Hope, she and the family went straight over there. There were so many of them that they entered through the back staircase with a little help from the guard.

Turn tried to sit up when he saw Hope; she asked him why. But he just hugged her. He couldn't find the words. Elsa came in next with tears gushing down her cheeks. She fell in love all over again and hugged her husband. He said to her, "Don't worry, girl, don't cry for me, I died years ago. I died when that van crashed." He turned to her and said, "Who are you?"

Elsa replied, "I am your wife."

"No, you were Ian Baxter's wife, I'm not him anymore, I've got the same name and same finger prints, but inside that guy died. He died that very same day. I am a changed man, I am someone else now." She stood by the bedside, her hand in his. She had always understood the makings of her best friend. One by one the rest of Ian and Elsa's children came through the door with their own families or partners. Turn just smiled. The family was reunited.

Magazines wanted exclusive interviews, chat shows wanted to view him first. Everybody was on his side, all except the great British judicial system. He had owned up to his crimes, he had nothing to hide, what he had done was for the best. Some thought it was excessive but the rest were happy for it to be legalised. He told his story many times. It went on for months and he never failed to mention his ghetto brothers, may they rest in peace. He didn't expose Aaron and Hacker, they hadn't been caught so why involve them? They had the rest of their lives to plan out, with this exposure they could be arrested for being accomplices.

He was labelled a great man, one that had helped many people. The centres, the cottages, he had repaired people's lives and asked for nothing in return. People wrote letters saying that he had found their loved one's murderer or abuser and dealt with it quicker than any police force or justice keepers could ever have done. He had inspired millions and reduced crime through his valiant efforts. He should not be punished.

It was at this point, with Turn on trial for the murders, his solicitor wanted him to say that Flame and Shadow did the killings but he would not tarnish their names. They were equal in this venture and he would be judged that way. Only God could judge them now. The trial went on for a month with the prosecution unable to find anybody who would speak against Turn and what he had achieved during his time here on earth. He was sentenced to 150 years by the judge's order. The jury didn't take part but due to Turn's guilty plea the judge had no choice but to let justice take its course.

Turn was nearing 50. He knew he would live out the rest of his days in prison and was resigned to the fact. He knew someone would continue with his legacy. When Turn arrived at his prison he was welcomed by the guards, who were all honoured to meet him. As he walked through the prison the inmates clapped and hailed their hero. He was like a godfather, walking with his head held high. His cell was kitted out, he had every facility available to him outside. They let his family visit and have gatherings in the yard. He lived like royalty although he didn't want to be treated any differently to the others. He just wanted to do his time. But they weren't having any of it. He was going to be there for the rest of his life so they intended to make sure he was comfortable.

Hope came to see him regularly. She would joke that when she wanted to talk to him she would always be able to find him now. This would make Turn chuckle. He would often lay in his cell at night thinking about what Hope said to him one day. She said, "If I had realised it was you I would never have given the orders to take you down, I'm so sorry."

Turn didn't want her to feel bad. He said, "Don't say that, you're a good and honest cop. I know if you were faced with the same challenge you would deal with it the very same way. I am proud of you."

It had been raining non-stop for two days. One of the

prisoners said this was the sign they were looking for. Turn looked at him and said, "What's going on?" They were going to carry out a big prison break; half the prison were going to attempt it.

Turn wished him good luck and walked back to his room but the prisoner followed him. He stopped Turn and said, "Listen, this is for you, you need to get out. You are no good in prison."

The next morning, Turn was nowhere to be found. He was not in his cell. None of the other prisoners could say what had happened, they were preparing their own break out. No one could have guessed that this would have happened. Turn had only been in prison for six months and was able to escape. His cell door was still locked. It must be magic, but was it? Nah, of course not! A guard and the warden went to get Turn during the middle of the sleeping hours. When he first arrived the warden invited him to his office; he had to see Turn, and he had to honour him. He too was one of the people to have written a letter to that infamous PO Box address. He had written that his daughter had been raped and murdered. When he received that letter back to say that the job had been done he felt his life had come back to him. That was over ten years ago and he still respected him. He showed Turn the letter, he even apologised for his actions, but there was no other way around it. The warden was proud of Turn, he had always wanted to meet him, and when he was shot down after saving those children Turn had done a deed that could not be topped. He had put his daughter's soul to rest. He couldn't bear the thought of him in prison, no matter how many creature comforts he was given. The warden knew nothing could compare with freedom. So he decided to let him go.

They never reported his absence. After a week of not being able to speak to Turn, Hope arrived at the prison wanting to see the warden. He was honest and explained to Hope why he had done it. She sat down and looked at her hands. She had lost her father again. *Why does he do this?* The warden comforted her.

"Your father is a great man, he has taught us all a lot, and in his chosen way of life he has given everything. You both fight the same battle but with different tools, this is your father's way. We must all salute him. "If you wish to report me, I will take my punishment with pride, for I know if you were to put me in the same situation I would have done exactly the same thing." That reminded Hope of what her dad said to her when she went to see him in the prison. She dried her tears and thanked the warden for his kind words and promised him she would not let this matter go any further. If there were any questions, she would tell them he had dealt with the situation.

Turn was at Blue River. Zinc had taken pride in his job, it was noticeable. The properties were beautiful and the resort was clean. He told Zinc he didn't want to be disturbed, he was to tell everybody that Turn had not been to the resort since it was first bought. Zinc honoured Turn's wishes. He needed to mourn the death of his brothers. Aaron and Hacker joined him and spent a few days just in each other's company. Nothing much was said, they just reminisced and felt good together. This was the first time Aaron had seen Turn since Hacker came into the office telling him what had happened. That day Aaron learnt a new side to Turn, he had always respected him but this had grown. He was an outstanding person who fell to his knees when Hacker told him Shadow was dead. His feelings for Turn were the same and he remained loyal. He was one of the brotherhood; he had trusted him. He would never dishonour his family.

When Hacker and Aaron returned to the UK, Turn remained in Jamaica and would disappear for a couple of days at a time. Jamaica was a lot more ruthless than the UK. Killing was easy and no one cared about the next man. He took out a few people but it didn't feel the same as there was no special operation, it was just raw killing; killing people who didn't care about life or death, they would do their crime and sit back. If they got caught, they got caught. He had to do it where it mattered, where it made a difference, where he could make change. He was going to make a move.

Before returning to the UK, Turn flew to America and met with a leading cosmetic surgeon, one who had requested his services many years ago. His face was completely altered; he almost didn't recognise himself, and all he could tell was his grin and his eyes. Turn was now ready to return to the UK. As he walked through customs, he shook his head, things hadn't changed. The newspapers printed pictures of Turn as they knew him, still reporting eagerly on his mysterious disappearance. He smiled.

Turn was not a man to show emotion or need but his first stop had to be the centre. This was where he and his crew were able to help change the minds of those who had been taught to believe that their lives were not their own. They believed that this left them with one option: to regress in order not to expect anything or have anything expected of them. Their new friends at the project showed them how to believe in themselves and help each other to grow. Turn loved that. When he arrived at the project he stood on the pavement and gazed at it. He felt triumphant. Aaron had been a solid partner and obviously taken every step to expand the headquarters. There were new buildings on either side with some appearing to be hostels and others looking like tutoring schools. He was impressed. Turn slipped through the automatic doors to find the place, as usual, was bright, open and very welcoming. He was wearing an African Caftan when a volunteer approached him. He put on a false African accent stating that he was just looking around. Hacker heard the voice as he walked up the spiral staircase. He was sure it sounded like Turn but when he looked over the banister, the face he saw didn't match. He continued up the stairs thinking of Turn and the way he looked. No one could tell him any different:

that was the voice of a man he loved and respected. He smiled as he looked down on the ground floor from the upper level. He may have changed his facial features but that walk was what Turn always joked about – 'bad man walk'. He made his way back down the stairs to where Turn was, quickening his pace with every step. Turn's presence was felt as he stood next to him. He turned to him and laughed, unable to believe it was him…and that accent, well, it was way too jester-like. He didn't have to say a thing. He looked deep into his eyes as he raised his hand, gave him a brotherly handshake and took him to the office to see Aaron. They talked about his new appearance and Hacker kept touching him, wanting Turn to say something, it was the only way he could truly tell it was him. It was completely different to what they knew, sort of out of place, but it was good to have the man back on side. The heat was back on, but Turn let them know it was part-time. "I'm going to chill for a while, do something simple, and see what my children are doing from afar," he explained. He was going to keep a low profile before the reign of terror began once more.

Lightning Source UK Ltd.
Milton Keynes UK
04 February 2010

149529UK00001B/6/P